The Summer Everything Changed

ALSO BY RUTH LERCHER BORNSTEIN

Butterflies and Lizards, Beryl and Me
(a novel)

The Sky and Me (essays)

The Dancing Man

That's How It Is When We Draw

The Seedling Child

A Beautiful Seashell

Brave Bunny

Little Gorilla

and many others

The Summer Everything Changed

Ruth Lercher Bornstein

WELLSTONE PRESS
Ashland, Oregon

FIRST EDITION

Printed in the United States of America

ISBN 978-1-930835-06-1

WELLSTONE PRESS
404 Wilson Road
Ashland, Oregon
www.wellstonepress.com

For my family

white coral bells upon a slender stalk;

lilies of the valley deck my garden walk.

oh, how i wish that i could hear them ring;

that will only happen when the fairies sing.

—Anonymous

Foreword

It was a summer of the war.

The summer of Rudi but mostly of that other boy.

The summer of Lilly, a girl I never met but who has always been with me.

It was the summer everything changed.

Part One

Memorial Day, May 30, 1943

Dear Brand New Diary!

My thoughts are all scrambled, my head is spinning with everything I need to say, I'm ready to spill it and I don't know where to start, so OKAY!

This is Me.

One little drop in the ocean.

Janet Kessler.

Going on sixteen years old.

Actually, I've never seen the ocean. I live in Elksburg, a small town in Wisconsin. I've never been anywhere far except Milwaukee.

Last night there was another dramatic scene with Mom. "You run around until all hours! People judge us! You have to behave better than the others! We're different from the others!" And so on and so on. Usually I'm afraid to answer back because then I get the silent treatment which is worse than any screaming. But this time I got up my nerve and yelled, "I didn't ask to be born into this family! And I'm not different from all the other kids! I'm just different from you!!"

Well! Enough of morbid stuff; on to a more cheerful subject. You're a big empty book given to me by my Aunt Pearl, and I'm going to tell you everything that happens. Everything that's in my heart, at least for this whole summer. In other words, the truth, the whole truth, nothing but the truth, so help me, God.

Oh, God, there I go again. I have to tell you that I have this habit of saying, oh God. Only, of course, in private, like now. But I mustn't forget to tell you about the parade. In case I forget how it was.

First of all, this morning I just had time to jump out of bed, struggle into my ancient red and white uniform and grab my clarinet. Downstairs, Dad was already at the kitchen table with his cup of coffee and cigarette, and with a finger to his lips. "We must talk softly," he whispered. "Your mother, from working late is very tired this morning." I looked at their closed bedroom door. She might be tired but she also didn't want to lay eyes on me. Not after last night's screaming.

"An all-American girl I have." My dad beamed at me. "Marching in an all-American parade."

"Daddy!" I shoveled in my rice krispies. I know I'm American."

Outside I saw he'd put up our big American flag on the flagpole without me, and I stood for a minute gazing up at it waving in the breeze. On River Street, I joined my best friends, Elaine, who plays the saxophone, and Mary Lou, who looked cute and perky in her skimpy drum-majorette uniform. The band began to get assembled, but by the time we were fully organized and in our places, it was sweltering out and every one of us was boiling. Still, we managed to lead the Memorial Day parade down River Street to Main, marching the mile or so to Eternal Rest cemetery, practically the whole time blasting out "Stars and Stripes Forever." With me, as usual, trying to keep in line while trilling on my clarinet, and tears welling up in my eyes.

We passed Dad standing in front of the embarrassing Summer Sale – Prices Slashed signs all over our Kesslers Dry-Goods Store front and cheerily waving a little American flag at me.

Outside Pischelmeyers drug store, I thought I saw him. Tall, blond crew cut. I pulled in my stomach and tried to march straighter. The boy turned, he wasn't Karl.

Behind me, Elaine hissed, "Change feet."

Because the band finished first, we stood at the gates of Eternal Rest Cemetery and watched the rest of the parade. There was a **Hats Off To Our Farmers Helping The War Effort float**, a **Buy More War Bonds** float covered in red, white and blue crepe paper; as well as a **Defeat The Enemy, Send The Japs and Nazis to Hell** float filled with servicemen on leave and boys who have signed up for the war.

Next came poor old Mr. Stubenbaker from down the block, pushed in a wheelchair. His legs were blown off in World War One. I cried even more when Eugene Wilson was wheeled up. He's only twenty years old and his legs were blown off somewhere in the Pacific in this war. His dad was pushing him.

The Boy Scouts marched up, followed by the old ladies of the Daughters of the American Revolution. Police Chief Donnelly, in his spiffed-up police car, had his siren going and Mr. Thorpe, the oldest man in town—he's over a hundred years old—our only veteran of the Civil War, rode with the mayor in the back of a flag-draped Model T Ford.

Finally, as always, up marched our World War One veterans, each one wearing (if possible) his old uniform, badges, and medals. Mary Lou yelled, "Hi, Daddy!" and waved at her dad. Elaine waved at hers. My eyes stung. My dad should've been asked to march; he was drafted into that war, too. On the German side, of course, but he couldn't help it. No one can help which country he was born in. You can't help which parents you were born to, either!

After the parade there were speeches at the cemetery. The band sat below the stage and I felt that prickle in my chest when grouchy Reverend Hoffeffer kept droning on about Jesus Christ losing his blood for our sins. But, later, when we blasted out "Nearer My God To Thee" I got choked up like I always do; I squeaked in the high notes, and Elaine in first chair woodwinds glared at me.

Oh my God, it's just come to me. I've finally figured out why I always blubber when we march. It's not only because of the war. And it's not only because of all the boys going off to fight. It's not even because of "Stars and Stripes Forever." It's the people coming together, it's us in the band playing our parts together, all of us making the music swell up, all of us equally important, nobody sticking out or different. It's the people watching us, and smiling and waving American flags at us and cheering us on. It's me being part of it all.

Back home, I tore off my sleazy uniform, smeared on my Red-Red lipstick, rubbed Mum deodorant under my arms, dabbed Evening In Paris colonge behind my ears, and squeezed into my new, aqua, princess-style dress. I've given myself a once over in my vanity mirror and, if I do say so myself, I look pretty good. Uh-oh, my ride just honked. More when I get back from the dance, I hope with exciting news. You know what I mean. He's sure to be there.

Dear Diary,

Oh God, I just looked at my clock. It's 3:00 p.m. the next day. I woke up at 11:00 a.m. but my stomach still felt like it was swimming in greasy alcohol so I turned over and went back to sleep. Now that I'm awake and feel a little better, I remember that I did promise to tell you everything so here's the whole sad story.

As you know, my ride honked and I ran outside and jumped into a guy's Model A Ford. That is, in the rumble seat, next to Mary Lou. Two minutes later, we were out of town, rattling past newly planted cornfields and long green pastures full of peacefully grazing cows and frolicky calves. Finally, after five long miles, with us screeching, "I'm a Yankee Doodle Dandy," we arrived at Eagle Lake.

I have to tell you that Eagle Lake is our lake, my friends and mine, our every-summer hangout with clear blue water that sparkles in the sun. And there's the Eagle Lake dance hall, it must be over a hundred years old. It has a stage and bands used to play here, but all we have now is a big, old jukebox in one corner.

Some boys who've just been drafted were standing around the jukebox slugging beer and singing "Don't Sit Under The Apple Tree With Anyone Else But Me" and this great sweep of feeling came over me, for the ones who'll have to go off to fight and maybe die, and even for those like me, left behind. If I'm soupy-sentimental I don't care. I wanted to kiss them all.

Some kids were already dancing on the scuffed wooden floor. Karl's pal, Morrie Fitzgerald, was slouched against a wall guzzling a bottle of hard stuff. I scanned the room.

He was there.

Our eyes locked. Oh, I wanted to throw my arms around him. But Karl's arms were busy. Karl's arms were around a tall, busting-out-of-her-low-cut-dress, flaming redhead.

Someone slapped another nickel into the jukebox. Frank Sinatra's soft voice floated out. "I'll be seeing you . . . " Karl smiled at me from over the girl's shoulder.

And before the song was over, " . . . that my heart embraces" . . . he and the girl slipped out the door. Frank Sinatra sounded almost as heartbroken as me.

The music changed, the next tune was a fast one and I glommed onto Mary Lou and swung her around. She untangled herself from me, so I grabbed Joyce, then Jean, then Shirley and twirled them like crazy. I flung myself all over the place. My face hurt from pretending I was having a swell time.

I ran outside and, in spite of myself, bought one of those giant hot dogs at the food stall, slobbered it with mountains of ketchup, mustard, and sauerkraut, and wolfed it down.

At Dicky's Dock next door, a rainbow of freshly painted canoes bobbed up and down. I wanted to leave, to escape, take a bright red canoe out on the lake and not come back. But the dance hall door swung open; "Praise the Lord And Pass the Ammunition" blared out from inside, and Mary Lou, along with two boys home on furlough, pulled me back into the hall. I know, keeping up the morale of our soldiers is the least I can do. But I still wish I'd taken off in the canoe by myself.

Soon, it seemed like everyone disappeared into cars, including Mary Lou, and I found myself alone in some soldiers' jalopy. The boys kept feeding me Southern Comfort whiskey and Virginia Dare wine.

After several swigs, I didn't mind the liquor's sickening-sweet taste. After several more, it hit me. I pushed open the car door and threw up the Coca-Cola and potato chips and the hot dog and everything else I'd eaten all day. On the way home, the boys had to stop the car so I could throw up again.

Naturally, standing at the front door in her flannel, all-weather nightgown, staring at me in horror, was my hands-in fists, purple-faced mother. Just in time to see me heave a splat of vomit at her feet. She pulled me into the house and slammed the door shut. Daddy was in the front room behind her, silent in his armchair, smoke swirling around him.

Then it came. "You're only fifteen years old and you're already getting yourself drunk? How many times do I have to tell you? People watch us! We have to behave better than the others!" The same old tirade. This time I didn't have the strength to scream back at her. I was barely able to crawl upstairs.

I'm sitting down at my vanity now, studying my hungover face in the mirror and trying a smile at myself. I do that a lot; I'm not sure why. Maybe it's because . . . as Dad always says, "It's better to laugh than to cry."

Dear Diary,

I'm looking down from my open, second-story window, and I see that old Mrs. Dickerson's blood-red roses are beginning to bud. Her hollyhocks are blooming, her bleeding hearts, her lilacs. Perfect white clouds are sailing in a perfect blue sky. And only two feet away, in Mrs. Dickerson's enormous elm tree, a mother robin is planted on her nest. No matter what, I have to admit that the world is breathlessly beautiful today.

My stomach is crying out for milk. More later.

I'm halfway down the stairs with you. I can hear them in the kitchen. "She's not a child anymore," Mom is saying. "I'm afraid . . . the way she came home, Sam. It's not so wonderful here as we thought it would be. We made a mistake moving here."

How could she say that about Elksburg? I just slid down to keep the stairs from creaking.

"To live here, a mistake?" That's Dad. "So soon you have forgotten? To move to this small place, you were the one who wanted it. To be independent. It is here we could forget the old country, start new. People here are good, Rachel. We work hard. They respect us."

I've heard the story. Both my parents came here after World War One. Daddy was working in a glove factory in Milwaukee when the great Depression happened, the factory closed down and Uncle Abe hired him to work in his clothing store. But Mom wasn't happy with that arrangement; she said it was like taking charity. So, somehow, when my folks heard about an empty store up north, they moved up here with hardly anything, to start a business and be on their own.

"We were alone then, Sam," Mom is going on. "Anywhere, the two of us could manage. But with a child . . . the bad influences here . . . ."

"Now, now," Dad interrupts. "Don't worry so much. That she came home sick, she just made a mistake, it was not her fault. You should have seen her, your all-American child marching in the all-American parade."

Silence from my mother.

"You will see," Dad says. "Everything will turn out for the best."

"All right . . . . But you know. You know as well as I do—little children, little problems . . ."

Not that again!

Daddy is chuckling. "Yes, I know. Little children, little problems, big children, big problems."

I've heard that one a few million times.

"And what of the news?" Mom's voice has risen. "The terrible . . ."

"Shhh . . . not so loud . . . ."

Why is he always shushing her? I just slid down more steps.

The newspaper rattles. There's no more talk. What was Mom going to say? What's so terrible? Besides me that is. Besides the war. I know I won't get an answer even if I ask. When I used to ask my mother how it was for her in the old country, she said that the past didn't matter, that her real life began when the boat sailed into New York Harbor and she saw the Statue of Liberty. My father mainly tells jokes to avoid the subject. They've never answered any of my questions.

I'm back in bed. As far as problems, Mom, I don't want any big problems, either. I just want to be what I feel like. And what I feel like . . . what I am, darn it, is just a plain old, typical, small town, Yankee Doodle girl!

Uh-oh, she's on my stairs.

My mother announced she's going to phone my Aunt Pearl. "I was ashamed to tell her about your terrible behavior but I hope they will agree to take you for the summer. In Milwaukee you will be away from bad influences."

All I could think of was: leave my friends? Give up days at the lake? And, hope against hope, give up forever on Karl?

"Also, don't think you will get off easy. From now on I'm going to watch you like a hawk. Starting next week, you will work in the store. Until then you are not to leave the house."

I yanked the covers up to my chin.

"Do you hear me? Not under any circumstances are you to leave the house until I say so."

There was no use arguing with her. If I don't make any smart remarks, she might change her mind about Milwaukee.

So all I said was, "Okay."

She still didn't leave. "The wash is done. I won't be home from the store until late. Now get dressed and hang the wash on the clothesline. When it's dry, take it off the line and iron everything."

I pulled the covers over my head.

Dear Diary,

She's gone at last and I'm down in the kitchen. I grabbed two pieces of bread from the breadbox, slathered them with butter and jam, then fortified myself with a bowl of Rice Krispies and milk to prepare for a couple of hours of answering letters from penpal soldiers, sailors, and Marines I don't know, but who are lonely, and pass along my name to other homesick guys.

Before I get up the energy to write the bunch of V-mail letters, and before I hang up the wash, I need something to cheer me up. I'm going to call up Elaine.

Elaine said she can't come over. She promised her mother she'd help bake rhurbarb pies for church, and then she has to cut up carrots and potatoes for tonight. "My grandparents from Deersville are coming to visit my great-grandparents' graves today and then they'll be over at my house for supper."

Elaine won't admit it but I know she likes that her mom is always home. I wouldn't mind a mother like hers, who doesn't have to slave at a store all day, who doesn't come home too tired to make a meal, who actually hugs and kisses her children and thinks they can do no wrong.

The phone. Elaine just called me back. The Red Cross needs us to knit a bunch of khaki-colored scarves for the soldiers. I said okay.

All at once, I'm tired of talking. Tired of the Red Cross and khaki-colored scarves. Tired of hearing about baking pies with mothers for church. Tired of people's grandparents coming over for supper. Tired of people having grandparents!

An old picture I used to draw just popped into my head; the daydream of me and my imaginary grandfather, the way I always thought of him, white flowing beard and all, just like in *Heidi*, my old, hand-me-down book from cousin Grace.

Tired of feeling sorry for myself!

The wall phone again. This time it was Mary Lou. Here's how our conversation went.

Mary Lou: "I saw Karl Kunkel this morning."

Me, my heart thumping: "Where?" (I forgot to mention that Mary Lou is the only person who knows.)

Mary Lou: "I bumped into him and Morrie Fitzgerald by the Farmer's Feed Co-op. And, you know what, Janet? I think Karl likes you."

Me: "He does not! Why do you say that?"

Mary Lou: "I saw the way he looked at you at the dance. Also, I asked him if he was going with anyone and he said no."

Me: "You didn't! What about that redhead?"

Mary Lou: "I just told you. He doesn't have a girlfriend."

Me: "You better not say anything to him about me!"

I was interrupted by a loud voice—her mother's—in the background. Mary Lou muttered, "Gotta go. I have orders to iron every sheet, every handkerchief, every sock!

I'm always surprised—and relieved—that a natural-born American like Mary Lou's mother, not only a foreigner from Russia like mine, thinks that you have to iron socks.

And Karl. If Mary Lou is right . . . and please God, make her right . . . then maybe I do have a chance with him.

I just reached under my pillow, pulled out my new 1943 yearbook and gazed at Karl's graduation picture. Under his handsome face, it says, "All the girls sigh when he goes by." Under that, he scrawled,

> ***To Janet, a cute kid and a good artist.***
> ***Be seeing** you around, Karl*

He must know how I feel about him. Once, in Study Hall, Karl intercepted a doodle I was passing to Mary Lou . . . a boy and a girl with their arms wound around each other . . . and from two rows away, he'd turned and mouthed, "swell drawing" and smiled at me, and I went red in the face.

I'm not sure exactly why I love him. I don't really know much about him. Maybe it's partly my motherly instinct. I loved him when he collapsed, all hot and sweaty with an agonized look on his face after losing the 400 yard dash. I wanted to comfort him when he fell all over himself trying to make a basket. Even though he's tall and gangly and has a blond crewcut, he reminds me of short, dark-haired Frank Sinatra. You know, needful of love.

And the way his electric-blue eyes bore through me when I asked him to sign my yearbook! His sidekick, Morrie Fitzgerald, tried to pull him away, but our fingers touched and I actually felt an electric thrill.

Boy, am I glad I have you to confide in, Dear Diary. I know everyone needs love. I just need it more. I hope I'm not abnormal.

Dear Diary,

I'm writing this later in my room. An almost-half moon was rising over Mrs. Dickerson's tree by the time I clumped downstairs, grabbed a box of Ritz crackers from the kitchen, and plopped down on the sofa. As usual, Mom was already in bed, and Dad was in his easy chair, the *Reader's Digest* on his lap, and his ear glued to the radio.

"My fellow Americans . . . " It was President Roosevelt's friendly voice. "We on the home front must spare no effort. We on the home front must give our all for the war."

After that it was "Hitler . . . Poland . . . Refugees." The ash from Dad's cigarette was dangerously close to falling. Then he noticed me and snapped off the radio. And I said to him, "Don't I know there's a war on? Aren't I a faithful correspondent to a whole army of servicemen?" He just smiled and told me that next was Jack Benny. "Always, my Janet, it is better to laugh than to cry." But his eyes were moist. My dad and I have a lot in common.

I just thought: Now that Karl's eighteen and has graduated he'll probably be drafted and I'll never see him again.

Dear Diary,

The morning light is dappling through Mrs. Dickerson's tree. The mother robin is still sitting on her nest, sort of like my mother sits on me. I just had a delicious daydream. Karl was a Navy Cadet in a smart white summer uniform and I was a Nurse Cadet. We met on the train going down to the Great Lakes Naval Station and we couldn't help it, we kissed passionately until we were torn apart. But of course we'd write.

Now I'm sprawled on my twin bed, surveying my room: the shelves crowded with umpteen drawing pads, scrapbooks, and years of every birthday card, every Christmas card, and every other holiday card I ever got. Mom calls my collections junk but I told her I need every single thing. At least she's given up nagging at me to throw everything out.

Drawings I've done of movie stars are pinned on a bulletin board Dad tacked up for me on my wall: a soulful portrait of Frank Sinatra I copied from a magazine; ditto Ginger Rogers dancing with Fred Astaire; ditto Clark Gable passionately embracing Scarlett O'Hara in *Gone With The Wind.* And, crazy as it is, but anyway no one else will ever see it, I just drew a picture of Karl and me in an even more passionate embrace.

There's a knock at my door. See you later.

It was Mom, of course. She wanted me to know that she's still keeping an eagle eye on me. I almost laughed. Today she's an eagle. Two days ago she was a hawk. She reminded me that she's waiting to hear from my Aunt Pearl about when I can go to Milwaukee. She also repeated that I'm still not allowed to leave the house until I start work at the store next Monday. But tonight she'd make an exception. But only for the world famous (joke) Methodist church supper. And I have to come home with them right after. Well, at least I'll get a real meal. More soon.

Dear Diary

It's after eleven p.m. After the church supper and the depressing movie. First, I'll try to explain (for posterity!) about church suppers. For instance, everyone who belongs to the Methodist church is part of one big family. Every lady cooks and bakes for you, especially if you're sick. Or dead. They also pray for you, especially if you're sick or dead. Elaine's mother greeted us downstairs at the entrance to the church social hall. "Hello, Mr. and Mrs. Kessler," she said to my parents. "How nice to see you." She only gave me a look. I could tell she knew I came home drunk last Saturday night.

As usual, the supper was baked ham, scalloped potatoes, and green and red jello salads with canned fruit along with my favorite dessert, Mrs Dickerson's famous apple pie with its side of cheddar cheese.

As usual, Mom was served chicken instead of ham; she's never even tasted ham. I've always laughed with Daddy about it. He's told me it's a left-over habit from the old country. Like bacon. It's supposed to be healthy for you so, even though it's rationed, Mom sometimes cooks it for me on Sundays, the whole time holding her nose. Of course, like everybody else, she saves the bacon fat to help make guns for the war.

Elaine's family are strong church goers. After they gave thanks and ate their supper, Elaine asked me to go to the movie show with her, but I told her I was still canned, my mother wouldn't let me go. Just then Mayor Macklin announced that in all of Elksburg, Mrs. Kessler (my mother, in case I forget!) has given the most blood for the war effort (I'm glad you have to be eighteen to give blood). People were clapping, so it seemed like a good time to ask. Dad immediately pulled out two quarters and told us to go and have a good time. Mom's face was red but she couldn't stop me with everyone watching.

The movie was not Ginger Rogers and Fred Astaire or some comedy. The movie was called, *Hitler's Children, The Real Truth About the Nazis.* And blazed across the screen—"The Way of Life in the Land

Where They Make Sure That Women Bear the 'Right Kind' of Children . . . or None at All. The Land Where a 'Master Race' is Planning to Make Slaves Out of Non-Aryan People Wherever They Are!"

Out on the sidewalk, Elaine asked me what was wrong, that my face looked kind of pinched. "You were scrunched down in your seat the whole time. And you didn't even finish your popcorn!" She grabbed my arm. "You always feel like you're the one getting killed. Jannie, it was only a movie!"

"I know." I dragged Elaine forward and said we should skip down the street like we used to.

"Right here?" she said. "Like little kids?"

I kept pulling her. "Please, Elaine, We're not grown-up women yet."

Good old Elaine. We held hands and skipped down Main Street, my shadowy shape in the store windows close to hers. We bounced past City Hall and its clock faithfully chiming the hour, and over the bridge with the street lights reflected on the river, past neighbors on front porches and in front rooms listening to the radio, past the dark shapes of familiar trees and familiar dogs barking, past crickets and fireflies with the moon keeping us company overhead. Holding hands and laughing and taking long, laughing skips to home.

Dear Diary,

My clock says 6:00 a.m. My heart's still pounding, the nightmare was so real. I was drawing a picture of my street, then, suddenly, it was dark, the picture came alive, and I was somewhere else, in a prisoner of war camp in Germany, cowering behind a barbed wire fence. Above me, I saw a B-17 bomber. There was an explosion, the plane was hit by Nazi cannons but the pilot managed to bail out.

Oh, dear God, the Sunday-Mass church bells are especially beautiful this morning. It's over. My Nazi nightmare is over.

Except for Karl Kunkel. I'm pretty sure he was going to save me in my dream.

Now that I'm totally awake, I realize it's quiet in the house, no newspaper rattling, no smell of coffee wafting upstairs. The folks are already gone to do their Sunday catch-up work at the store and they won't be home until dark. All my friends are busy today, Mary Lou at Mass, Elaine helping with little kids at the Methodist church, and everyone else at every other church in town.

And me? I've made up my mind. I'm going to escape to my favorite place in the world.

Dear Diary,

Boy, am I glad I took you with me. My adventure began when I shoved an apple, bread, and cheese packed in wax paper into my knapsack, walked the two blocks to the edge of town, and stuck out my thumb. I was picked up by a nice old farm couple who had to get home after early Mass to milk their cows.

At the turn-off to the lake, I thanked them, hopped out, and walked the rest of the way. I passed a mailbox: KUNKEL'S FARM (thump, thump) and kept looking around, half-expecting Karl to jump out from behind a cornstalk.

At Dicky's Dock, I plunked down a quarter for Dick, chose a paddle from those hanging on the wall, stepped into a red canoe, and pulled away onto the lake. Once I was on the silky-blue water with the smooth motion of the paddle under me and the sky so blue over me, everything sad seemed to float away.

I paddled past the pines and the cottages surrounding the lake, past a fisherman in a rowboat and a few people in canoes. At the far end of the lake, I saw a narrow passageway I'd never explored before. Trees on either side of the inlet hung over the water and a snowy-white egret at the entrance let me paddle close. I made my way in, bumped up against a tiny island, and the egret spread out its wings and flew over me.

I pulled off my shoes, stepped into the chilly water—tiny minnows tickled my toes—and hauled the canoe up on the rocks. I tramped past a clump of birches and settled myself under a trembly leafed aspen.

The only sounds here are the soft lapping of waves and the sighing of wind in the trees. I wonder if anyone has ever been in this exact spot before me. I just took a very long, deep breath.

And caught a whiff of something sweet.

Poking up out of last year's moldy leaves, are delicate, pure-white lilies of the valley. And suddenly, that feeling I used to have, is back—when I was sure I was connected by an invisible thread to trees, to flowers, to every living thing. When I loved everything, wanted to touch everything. When I was sure everyone I met was related to me. When I thought everyone was related to everyone else.

That was before I got so mixed up, one minute happy, the next minute, sad. One minute dying to be with my friends and the next minute, like now, glad to be alone. Before I realized that I wasn't the same as my friends. And, of course, before the war.

Something amazing just happened. An ant was dragging something past my toes, something as big and beautiful as blue stained glass. I bent closer and saw that it was a torn-off part of a dragonfly wing. Suddenly an enormous, shiny, cellophane-blue dragonfly zoomed past me, then zig-zagged around me again, as if he was saying, "Don't look down there! Look at me! Aren't I gorgeous? All I do every day is flit around trees and flowers. Look at me, I'm alive!"

I leaned against the tree and closed my eyes. I almost felt that I was the dragonfly, that I was part of the grass and the rocks, the sky and the water all around me. And then, as always, for some unknown reason, Helen Keller popped into my mind. She'd love it here. She could smell the flowers, but she couldn't see the dragonfly, she couldn't even hear it buzzing. And how could I describe to her the colors of the light on the dragonfly's wings?

I opened my eyes. A second dragonfly has attached itself on top of the first one and they're zooming around me together. Are they "doing it?" How could I tell Helen Keller about that?

But oh, Dear Diary, I know I should be used to being an only child, but more than ever I wish I had a sister; even better, a twin sister. We'd be here together talking about the light and Helen Keller, and giggling about the dragonflies. Or we'd be lying on our twin beds drawing pictures or complaining about Mom always haranguing us. Or talking about how much we want love.

If I had a sister, I wouldn't be the only Jewish kid in town.

Like at Easter sunrise service with Mary Lou. The church was so beautiful with all the lights and candles, and I felt beautiful singing all the hymns. But then, after the service, (the priest preached about the crucifixion of Christ) a kid cornered me and spouted that his family was going to heaven and my family was going to burn in hell, and when I asked him why, he said it was because we killed Jesus, and my face flamed up and I wanted to smack him one, but I couldn't because he's only seven. I felt a little funny later, sauntering down Main Street with my friends, wearing my new pink Easter suit and the pink hat I made, really pretty with a veil and artificial roses.

Or that time, shopping for records in Appleville with Elaine and her mother. Out of nowhere I heard someone say, "She tried to Jew me down," and I swirled around, and Elaine heard it too, but all she said was, "Forget it. She didn't mean anything by it, it's just the way people talk."

"Sticks and stones will break your bones, but words will never hurt you." I tried to push down the words I heard, deep down, out of sight. And I do. Most of the time.

But then, just last week, I heard Elaine's grandmother say, "That little Jewish girl." I never hear anyone say, "that little Catholic girl" or "that little Methodist girl" or "that Lutheran girl." Maybe there is something not quite right about me. But, of course, I'd never admit that to Mom.

The dragonfly is hovering over me again, He's staring at me with his many eyes. What does he see? It's almost as if he knows how I used to feel. How I want to feel now. That maybe there really is an invisible thread between me and world.

Dear Diary,

I tried to hang on to that good feeling I had on my secret island, but today I had to start work at our store, which was not too bad because of what happened just before we closed. You didn't think I'd forgotten about "you know who," did you?

There's been a sign in our store window since the war began.

Remember Our Boys In The Service
Alterations Free Of Charge
Buy War Stamps With The $ You Save

Propped up in a corner is a smaller sign:

The Customer Is Always Right

It's like we have to beg for people's business, always have to have sales, like two-piece bathing suits, "Below Cost for Quick Clearance," and maternity dresses that were $2.98, now selling for $2.23. Anything to get customers inside. Today I was artistically arranging the socks, handkerchiefs, and underwear by color and size, when Mrs. Shweiner barged in, mangled my whole display, and didn't buy a thing. To make up for it Mom let me try on several just-in Newest Style rayon blouses as well as a pretty cotton flowered dress that Mom said she'll only have to alter a little to make it fit me perfectly.

But at least there was something different this afternoon. A whole slew of Negro men wandered into the store. Mrs. Schweiner, who was pawing through some dresses, glared at them and stalked out; Dad just shook his head at her back, smiled his sad smile, said, "Welcome," to the men, and handed each one a hankie, for free.

And then, as if on cue, just like in a movie, Police Chief Donnelly strode in. He thanked the men for coming all the way from Jamaica. "What with the war and the shortage of locals and all," he told them, "we sure needed lots of help with the crops." The workers smiled politely, and I tried not to stare. I wondered if their skin felt different.

After the workers left (they bought a few pairs of socks), Dad asked the chief if there was anything he could do for him. Believe it or not, the Chief said he only stopped in to get cheered up by one of my dad's jokes. Dad's grin was so wide he looked like he was going to burst. Here it is, in case I could ever forget. My dad's *Reader's Digest* joke.

"A salesman gave up his job and joined the police force. A friend asked him how he liked this new job. Well, the policeman said, besides the pay and the hours, you know what I like best about the new job?"

Dad gave a long pause. The chief and I bent forward.

"It's that the customer is always wrong!"

Chief Donnelly roared. Dad laughed so much at his joke that tears ran down his cheeks.

"Now, folks," said the chief, "if you'll excuse me, I gotta round up some gol darn Nazis that've swarmed into town."

What? I looked at Dad. He was lighting up a cigarette; he was laughing. Oh, of course. It was a joke. There could never be any danger here.

And then—here it comes—just before we locked up, Morrie Fitzgerald peered into the store. I looked past him out the open door, and there, out on the sidewalk, big as life, was Karl! Standing there with his blond head outlined by the street light, and with his hands in his back blue jean pockets. I was sure he could hear my heart clanging away.

Dad motioned to me that a customer was waiting. I rang up the sale, then peeked out behind the "Remember Our Boys" sign.

Karl was gone.

From Richter's bar next door, Frank Sinatra crooned . . . "I'll be seeing you . . ."

There was something about the way Karl had looked at me.

". . . that my heart embraces . . . ."

Something.

Dear Diary, am I only imagining that Karl's look meant something more than just a look?

Dear Diary,

It's two days later. I was drying the dishes when the mailman rang. Here's the letter Mom got back from Milwaukee:

> *Dear Rachel,*
> *As you know, Grace's husband has been sent overseas and Grace has come home to wait for her baby to be born. We will all be glad to have Janet's company. Right after the Fourth of July will be fine.*
> *With fond regards,*
> *Pearl*

"Two weeks," I said to my mom. "No more."

Then it started. "Not everyone is as lucky as you to be able to travel and visit your relatives. There are people in the world who would love to trade places with you. People who are forbidden to travel, who dress in rags, who have no home, no family, no place even to hide." And on and on and on!

All I did was say, "Mom, what's the matter? I know things are bad in Europe, but what does that have to do with me? I just happen to like my hometown, that's all."

But that only made her madder. "There is more to the world than this town! And there are other things to do this summer than run around until all hours, getting yourself drunk and doing I don't know what all with the boys!"

What does she think I do with boys, anyway? Doesn't she know I'd never do "It"?

And then, to top off her whole fit, she called me spoiled rotten. I tore off my apron, threw down the dish towel, and ran out of the kitchen.

"I am not spoiled!" I screamed from the front door, "And . . . and if I am, it's not my fault! It's not my fault you always let me have new dresses. It's not my fault Dad always sticks up for me. If I'm spoiled, it's your and Dad's fault!"

And it is!!

I ran across the street, grabbed a swing at the grade school playground. Some little kids on the swings stared at me, but I didn't care. I pumped as hard and high as I could.

Goodnight!

Dear Diary,

I'm writing this in bed. It's another muggy day. I have the curse and pretty bad cramps (being a woman means leading a hard life, and what's it like having a baby!?!), so I begged off work and phoned my friends to come over for a gabfest.

Okay, to back up a little, I was in the doghouse (Mom's famous silent treatment) for two days because I yelled back at her. Dad tried to make peace with, "Rachel, she's only a child." And with another of his favorite sayings, "Everything will turn out for the best."

Everyone else's mothers are home all day, so they always want to be at my house. Mary Lou, Jean, and Shirley each brought Lucky Strike cigarettes pilfered from their dads, Joyce brought Hostess Cupcakes, and I found some of Dad's left-over Manischevitz wine. And, of course, serious Elaine brought part of the afghan we're supposed to be knitting for the Overseas War Relief to send to poor refugees in Russia.

Naturally, the main topic was boys. Mary Lou told us about the "emotional impulses" she got when she was necking in the last row in the balcony at the Royal with some boy or other. She let us try on her new, very dark, maroon lipstick. It's guaranteed not to come off, no matter how long or hard you kiss. It burned our mouths but most of us want to get it. We were interrupted by Elaine who tried to change the subject. "Let's promise right now to finish our afghan."

I groaned along with the others. "It'll never be done."

"Well, then we should help with the next old clothes drive."

"No one has any old clothes left."

Well then, let's make more fudge to send to the soldiers."

That we agreed to. We also promised not to eat any fudge ourselves.

"And now," Mary Lou again, "What about boys . . . ?"

"No!" From Elaine. "Now we should discuss what we're going to be after we graduate from high school and are fully grown up."

Naturally, Elaine went first. She wants to join the Nurse Cadets, and if the war is still going on, she'll race to the front and nurse the wounded. Shirley and Jean and Joyce want to be nurses, too. Mary Lou can't decide whether she wants to enlist in the war as a Wac in the army or a Wave in the Navy, or be a professional dancer like Ginger Rogers, or be an Arthur Murray dance instructor, or work in an aircraft factory and put finishing touches on B-24 bombers, or get married right after high school and have lots of kids or if all else fails . . . she kept us waiting . . . a nun!

After we calmed down from our hysterics Elaine said that I definitely should be a nurse. "You're so smiley and friendly to everyone Jannie, and so soft-hearted, you always cry in movies and when we march, and you didn't even want to swallow that live minnow last summer."

But I didn't tell them what I want to be.

Which is: I don't want to grow up.

Uh-oh, Helen Keller just came into my mind! Look at what happened to her! It makes me ashamed that I can't stop needing love or even stop complaining. But it's true! I never want to get any older than I am right now. And I'm young for my age!

I am mixed up. If I want to get married and have a family of my own I'll have to grow up whether I want to or not. But when you're old you have to worry about who you're going to marry, and, of course, when I do, I'll probably break Mom's heart. And I don't want the problems Mom and Dad have, struggling so hard to make a living and having ungrateful kids like me.

The world is so complicated. But I'm not going to give up on myself.

I just got up and smiled at my face in the mirror.

Dear Diary,

At last! Exciting news! This morning, before work, on an errand to the five and ten cent store to buy Dad some cigarettes, I walked past the Farmer's Feed Co-op, not expecting anything, just looking at the cracks in the sidewalk, when someone said, "Hi Janet."

I stopped. It was him! Standing over me, looking down into my eyes. With those eyes.

"Oh, hi Karl." I stared up at him like an idiot. His blond crewcut has grown out a little. He was even more beautiful than I thought.

He threw a sack of livestock feed into an old, gray, beat-up pickup truck and got into the driver's seat. I just stood there. He started up the motor, then stuck his head out the car window. He smiled and said, "Be seeing you." And then, before he drove off, he blew me a kiss.

I was cemented to the sidewalk, my knees turned to mush.

Dear Diary,

Mrs. Dickerson's hollyhocks are taller than I am. At the edge of town the cornfields are changing, growing fast. "Knee high by the Fourth of July," Mrs. Dickerson says. Time is running out. I've got to do something before I'm banished to Milwaukee, something now, something that will make things change between Karl and me. Because I just thought, *The Fourth of July is only seven days from today*!

Dear Diary,

It's midnight on the Fourth of July. You're not going to believe what I did today. The desperation I felt. The guts I had. And what happened because of it. It still feels like one of my "lost for love" daydreams.

Here's how it all began: This morning I dragged out my clarinet (I hadn't picked it up since Memorial Day), pulled on my uniform, slurped up my Rice Krispies, helped Dad run up our American flag in the front yard, then ran down the block to meet the rest of the band.

After we marched downtown, blasting out "Stars and Stripes Forever" with my eyes blurry and all of Elksburg watching, after the parade was over and my folks were still at the Mothers for Christian Service bake sale, I rushed home, shucked my uniform, plastered on lipstick, rubbed Mum under my arms and Evening in Paris behind my ears, and pulled on my new blue shorts.

My hand shook as I took the receiver off the hook; my voice nearly gave out asking the operator to connect me to Kunkel's farm.

A lady answered and I asked if I could please speak with Karl (I sounded squeaky). The lady said he wasn't there and who was I.

My throat closed up. "A friend," I squawked.

"A friend? What friend? What's your name?"

"Just tell him I'll be at the lake." And I hung up.

Before I could get cold feet, I packed my knapsack with bread, cheese, and apples in wax paper and left a note on the kitchen table: "Be home soon."

The cornstalks rustled in a cold wind that suddenly came up, white clouds turned dark, and there was a far-off rumble of thunder. Luckily, I was picked up by a farmer who took me almost the whole way. I imagined Karl at the dock, his hair tousled in the wind, waiting for me.

At Dicky's Dock, there was no sign of him. I marched back and forth, shivering in the cold, willing him to come.

I stopped pacing. What a numbskull! I could have shot myself! How could he possibly have known it was me on the phone? And even if his mother had told him about the call, even if he had guessed it was me, why on earth would he come? I was nuts, crazy. The whole thing was crazy; was there ever such a knucklehead as me?

I went inside the dock office. Dick, the dock owner, sat in his office, his feet up on the desk. "It's choppy today," he said. "Sure you wanna go out?"

Oh, hell. I nodded. I'd paddle out to my island; maybe the egret would be there, maybe the dragonfly, maybe even some of the lilies of the valley would still be under the aspen tree.

I paid Dick my quarter, he shook his head and handed me a life preserver, and I untied the red canoe and tried to pull away from the dock. It was a struggle to fight the wind.

All at once, "I'll Be Seeing You" drifted out from the dance hall. Someone had put a nickel in the jukebox.

I looked over my shoulder. A boy was standing on the dock. Tall. Blond crew cut. My legs, even my arms, felt instantly weak. He motioned for me to turn the canoe around, and helped me stumble onto the dock.

"How . . . how did you know it was me?"

He said he just knew. He said he was glad I had the guts to call him up. He said he's been thinking about calling me up. You can imagine my joy. And shock!

Fat drops of rain began to spatter down and he led me under some tall trees near his pickup truck. I wanted to pinch myself to make sure this was real. That this was really Karl's arm, smooth and solid, around my waist. Under the trees we were sheltered from the rain. He bent over me. I closed my eyes. He kissed me. His lips were soft and warm. I kissed him back. He held me. I held him back. I breathed in his manly aftershave lotion. He practically had to hold me up.

The sky grew dark, the rain came down harder, and we dashed into his truck. He reached for me and I had to tell him, that rain or shine, I had to be home to get ready for the Fourth of July fireworks celebration tonght. In fact I had to tell him a few times. On the way home I racked my brain for something more to say.

I told him he was lucky to live near the lake. He answered that with all the farm work he had to do he didn't have much chance to go canoeing. Then he burst out that he wants to join up and be a pilot on a B-24 bomber, but the draft board keeps putting him off, keeps saying they need farmers to keep on growing corn.

Thank you, God. I said I was sorry.

Too soon we were at my house. Karl pulled me to him. The front room's curtains moved, my dad peered out the window. I had to tear myself away. I opened the truck door and stepped out. My legs were trembling.

"Tomorrow, Janet." He leaned out of the truck window, "Tomorrow night."

My heart nearly stopped. "Tomorrow I won't be here! I'll be gone! To Milwaukee!"

He pulled his head back into the truck.

"But it's only for two weeks!"

His hands were on the steering wheel.

"I'll be home very soon! In two weeks. I will!"

"Okay, guess I'll have to wait, then."

He started up the motor. "Be seeing you, Janet."

I stood in the rain and watched him turn the truck around, watched him drive down the block and turn right onto River Street.

Watched him disappear.

Before Mom could yell at me, I ran up the stairs, tore off my wet clothes, fell on my bed, and hugged my pillow. I touched my lips. His lips had pressed mine, his mouth had been on my mouth. It was a hundred times better than my drawings of us, a thousand times better than any of my daydreams. I'll never forget how his arms felt around me.

Dad yelled that I'd be late so I had to drag on my uniform, rub on fresh lipstick, dig out my clarinet again, and dash downstairs to grab the peanut butter and jelly sandwich Dad had ready for me. Dad said he'd see me at the park by the river but Mom, as usual, was too tired and was going to bed.

By some miracle, the rain stopped and the sky cleared. At the park, the main speech was by old Reverend Hoffeffer again, about how we Americans believe in the natural goodness of man, also that God is superior to man, and that we Americans are superior to everybody else; something like that. And then, of course, how our boys will come home from the war stronger in their Christian faith.

All during the rest of the speech and the boom and lights of the fireworks . . . red, white, and blue over the river . . . while we in the band blasted out "Yankee Doodle Dandy" and "God Bless America," I kept my mind fixed on Karl.

"Be seeing you," he'd said. Oh, please let him mean it. All through the noise of kids letting off firecrackers and the lights of swirling sparklers, I prayed, please God, let him love me.

Part Two

Dear Diary,

I'm on the train going down to Milwaukee. The first thing I did this morning (I hardly slept) was pack my yearbook (with Karl's picture) in the bottom of my suitcase. The second thing I did was write a note to Mary Lou. Here's what it said:

You're not going to believe this! Karl and I met at the lake. He's a man of few words but words weren't nesessary because we kissed and, oh!! it was more thrilling than I ever imagined. I can't tell you all the details now—remember this is just between you and me . . . but please call him up and tell him my address in Milwaukee which you can get from my mother.

I shoved you and my drawing pad into my knapsack, then took a quick look in the elm tree to say goodbye to the baby robins. The nest was empty. Mrs. Dickerson came out her front door, and by the delicious chocolaty smell coming out of the brown paper bag she carried, I could tell it was full of her chocolate chip cookies. "To give you strength," she said, giving me a squeeze, "for the long journey to Milwaukee." Mom handed me the lunch she packed and warned me that I must be on my best behavior; I must help Aunt Pearl, I am to ask permission before I go anyplace. She looked so worried I felt a little sorry for her.

Finally, Mary Lou and Elaine ran over to see me off. I slipped Mary Lou my letter, and Dad carried my suitcase to our old black Ford. I got into the front seat and looked back at everyone waving me off.

I kept looking back, looking back, till we were far out of town.

At Appleville train station some sailors heading south to the Great Lakes Naval Station got on the streamliner with me. A couple of the guys asked me to sit with them and, of course, I was friendly and smiled back at them, but I went straight to a solitary seat by the window. On the train platform Daddy waved at me and I waved back. The train began to move. Dad yelled, "A good time! A good time have for yourself, my Janet!" He looked teary. Like me.

I sat back. Two long weeks!

But Karl will still be there. My island will still be there. I'll write to Karl; I write good letters. Meanwhile, all I can do is get out my drawing pad and make another picture of Karl and me under the aspen tree and surrounded by lilies of the valley. Which I just did.

Now we're chugging past huge expanses of corn higher than my knees, past big red barns and silos, and green fields full of grazing cows and their calves, heavier and not as frisky as a month ago. We're swaying by blue lakes and dense-dark forests, by small towns like mine, with their City Halls, church steeples, and Farmer's Feed Co-ops. We rumble past a woman and a little girl standing by the tracks. The woman is holding the girl's hand. The girl is wearing a pink ruffly dress.

I think I remember holding my mother's hand the first day of kindergarten. And I used to have a cute dress like that, too. I might still have it in my closet. Mom made all my clothes back then. Back when I was sweet and little and didn't talk back.

Oh, God, I just dug into the bag for a cookie.

According to my gold watch (a present from Uncle Abe) we've only been traveling an hour. Three more long hours to go. Looking through you, Dear Diary, I see there's isn't much of anything about me; I mean nothing about how I look and how I always used to flip up my nose to make it pug like Mary Lou's, but I've resigned myself and anyway, my nose is straight and not too bad. My hair is kind of a reddish-darkish-blondish and is helped by nightly curlers (until now; I forgot to bring my curlers with me) and I'm on the short side and a tiny bit pudgy. All in all, I look like any other small town girl.

Oh well, time for another cookie. Is my lipstick still on? Is any chewy cookie stuck on my teeth? I just took my compact out of my purse and bared them. Teeth okay. I forgot to mention that my teeth are white enough and straight. I also applied more of my almost used up Red-Red lipstick.

Now the train is clanging into another station and more people are getting on. A woman has sat down next to me so I'm trying not to chew my cookie too loudly. I glanced at her sideways; she reminds me of Mom; small, round, with her hair pulled back in a bun. She's fingering a rosary and murmuring a prayer in another language. I never heard my mother speak any language but English. Except once. She was standing at the stove and didn't know I'd walked into the kitchen. The language was strange and soft; the melody was sad and beautiful. Why did she stop singing when she saw me?

A picture of my mother has popped into my head. Bent over, pedaling away on the old sewing machine at the store. Oh lordy, I just grabbed another cookie.

A couple of minutes ago, the train whistled and pulled into the next station and the lady with the rosary got off. What is Karl doing this minute? Is he thinking of me? I noticed a tattered sign: "*Gone With The Wind,*

The Greatest Moving Picture Ever Made," with a picture of Scarlett O'Hara and Rhett Butler in their passionate embrace. The kiss with Karl could be the close of a great, heartaching, romantic movie. But in real life, a kiss can't be the end. There has to be much, much more to come.

Dear Diary,

I'm writing this at night, under a pink, silky quilt at my aunt and uncle's house. This upstairs spare room has a soft green rug, a full length mirror on the closet door, and a white lamp that showers the room with a soft light. Shelves are full of books about art, and next to the bed, is a big tome called *America, the Melting Pot of the World.*

Aunt Pearl is modern—not like Mom. Not only was she born in this country, she plays golf and has a tan. Also, she doesn't have to work at their clothing store anymore, so she has time to make supper every night.

Downstairs there's a real Persian rug on the floor, the armchairs are covered with emboidered cloth, and pretty lamps are everywhere. Instead of the rickety end tables Dad got by sending in Raleigh cigarette coupons, a glass coffee table with carved feet stands in front of a velvety, pink-flowered sofa. Instead of *Saturday Evening Post* covers and Pischelmeyer drugstore calendars on the walls, they have paintings of flowers and beautiful ladies in Paris.

I kind of feel like a fish out of water but I promised to tell everything, so I'll start at the beginning. Cousin Grace was waiting for me on the Milwaukee train platform. She looked elegant and skinny, not at all like she's going to have a baby. We'd have dinner when we got home, she told me, but she must have a ham sandwich that minute.

In the station coffeehouse, I asked her if I could order apple pie with cheddar cheese. "Of course," Grace said, "whatever you want." She picked up her sandwich, made a face, and put it down. "When you're "expecting," she pushed her plate toward me, "you can suddenly feel sick to your stomach and you can't eat a thing." Really? I wished there was something that would make me stop eating. I ate Grace's sandwich as well as my apple pie.

After showing me a picture of her husband, handsome in his Army uniform, Grace asked me if I had a boyfriend. I pulled out my drawing pad and showed her a sketch of Karl. "Very nice," she said and then she flipped through the rest of my drawings. I was embarrassed at all the robins and dragonflies with human faces as well as the pictures of Karl and me kissing, but Grace just smiled.

Driving through downtown, horns blared, traffic lights changed on almost every corner, and the crowds of people on the streets all hurried past each other, going about their business. Not like at home where you know almost everybody and almost everybody knows you and you do not pass a person without saying hello. Another thing, wherever you looked there were hordes of soldiers and sailors. Something to tell boy-crazy Mary Lou.

At home, the first thing Uncle Abe did was pinch my cheek (so hard it hurt) and asked, "How is my favorite niece?" I winced and it wasn't only because of the pinch. As long as I can remember, he's always said I'm his favorite niece; it's his little joke since I'm his only niece. "Just look at this shaina maidele." He stood back, smiling. "Look how blond, how pretty. Just like a shiksha she looks." I remember the old country words (my only Yiddish words) from my last visit here (I think I was twelve). "Shaina maidele" means pretty girl. "Shiksha" means a gentile, non-Jewish girl. I'm glad about that but it still gives me that weird, mixed-up feeling. Does that mean Jewish girls aren't supposed to be pretty?

Supper was served with two forks and was some kind of fish I've never had before, along with a sauce and slices of lemon on the side. We also had a vegetable called asparagus. After dessert—big slabs of apple strudel brought home by my uncle—we drifted into the front room and sank into the easy chairs.

"The Germans are on the offensive on the Russian front," the radio announcer told us. "The Russian people are suffering, but putting up a brave fight." The same news as at home. Except their radio is fancy and stands all by itself on the floor.

Aunt Pearl asked me what I'd like to do for the short time I'd be with them. I didn't know what to answer and she suggested that I might want to meet some people my age, and that she knows a nice boy. "He's the nephew of friends of mine, he doesn't know any young people here and, any day now, he'll be leaving to join the armed forces."

The armed forces? I felt disloyal to Karl but I had to say okay.

My aunt sprinted to the phone. "Rudi's already in the army?" I heard. "First in line at the enlistment center? He couldn't wait?" She seemed very disappointed. Not me. The thought of acquiring still another correspondent makes me feel tired.

So here I am, Dear Diary, under this silky quilt, already homesick and gazing at Karl's picture in my yearbook.

Karl, please write to me!

Dear Diary,

A strange day. In fact, a lousy day. After breakfast, Aunt Pearl led me into the living room, sat me down on the couch, put a soft pillow behind me, opened a leather photo album and showed me a snapshot of my parents taken just before they got married. Mom's arm is around Dad and she's actually smiling.

I know the rest of the pictures of my family. We have the same ones, and they're mostly of me. Me, very cute at age one, pouting at age two, posing with smiles at age four. My parents have photographs of me at every stage.

I stared at a faded brown photograph I'd never seen before. It showed my mother in the old country, together with about seven other girls, all in long dark dresses and looking very seriously at the camera. I asked why there weren't more pictures of Mom and Uncle Abe when they were kids.

Aunt Pearl told me their family was poor; they didn't have enough money in Russia to have many photographs taken. She went on to say that Uncle Abe came here alone when he was only sixteen (I already knew that) and he worked at odd jobs and saved up his money till he could be on his own. He brought his little sister, my mother, over after the Great War (which I knew) and he still works hard to give his family the kind of life he could only dream of in the old country.

Aunt Pearl is very different from Mom. She likes to talk.

She told me she'd never seen anyone so determined to learn English as my mother; she refused to speak even a bit of Yiddish or Russian. Not a word of Polish or German, either. I was surprised and said to my aunt that I didn't know Mom spoke all those languages.

"Your mother didn't tell you?"

I leaned forward. Aunt Pearl was going to tell me something.

"Your mother didn't tell you that during the first World War their little Russian town was overrun, first by the Germans, then by the Poles?"

I felt like saying, "No, my jolly mother doesn't say anything much about anything except to harangue me that I have to behave better than my friends."

From now on, Dear Diary, I'll try to record every word. It might be important information.

Aunt Pearl: "But the Russian Cossacks were even worse."

Me: "What are Cossacks?"

My aunt looked even more surprised. "You haven't heard about the terrible Pogroms?"

Me: "Pogroms?"

My aunt bit her lip. "Never mind, Janet. Now, what would you like for lunch?"

But it didn't end there.

After lunch, scrambled eggs filled with mushrooms and cheese, which she called an omelette, my aunt sat me down again. "You're old enough," she said. "And I've decided it's time. I'm going to take it upon myself to tell you about your family's history. And first I'm going to tell you about the Russian Cossacks and their Progoms."

I didn't want to hear about Russian Cossacks and the Pogroms.

"When times were hard, and even when they weren't, the Cossacks, as well as some of the local peasants, with their stomachs full of vodka, rode their horses through your mother's village, shouting, cursing, looting, killing." My aunt gave a long sigh and looked away. "And assaulting . . . raping . . . young Jewish girls."

Me: "Oh." I kept my eyes on the painting of a beautiful girl in Paris. But then I had to ask. "But Mom and Uncle Abe, and their parents, weren't they Russian, too?"

Aunt: "They were Russian Jews."

I felt that chill. "What do you mean?"

"All I can tell you is that the Jews were blamed for whatever might be—or might not be—going wrong. They couldn't own property in that town, their children couldn't go to public schools. Our people weren't allowed to farm or work at most professions. They had to keep to themselves for safety's sake, had to do whatever they could, like peddling, to survive."

I only stared at her.

"Your uncle," my aunt bit her lip again, "he won't like it that I talked to you about this; he doesn't like to look back. Please don't tell him about our conversation."

Me: "I won't." I got myself up from the soft couch. She doesn't have to worry about that!

It still wasn't over. My aunt put out her hand. "About your mother. I can't blame her for wanting to forget the old country, the old ways. But to live in such a small town with no other Jewish families?"

"Please Auntie Pearl," I answered. "I'm glad my folks live in Elksburg. Now, may I be excused?"

Uncle Abe brought home corn beef and pastrami, spicy mustard, heavy rye bread with pumpernickel seeds, herring in sour cream and kosher dill pickles, and for dessert, bakery-fresh slabs of apple strudel. And he and I ate and smiled at each other and patted our full stomachs as if nothing in the world was ever wrong.

Dear Diary,

It's 2:00 a.m. Why do I have to be a "people?" Why can't I just be me? I didn't want to hear that they had to keep to themselves. I didn't want to hear about peddling to survive and how awful it was to be Jewish.

I hate that word, Jew. I hate the word Gentile, too, but "Jew" gives me the creeps; it's so ugly and hard-sounding. Are we really so different from other people? Is that why I have an afraid feeling when I hear the word Jew? It's almost as if we're not as human as the others. And about Russia! It's all so queer. We love Russia so much now, Russia is our brave ally in the war. I don't understand a bit of it.

I just got out of bed. My old friend, the moon, as beautiful and mysterious as ever, is smiling down at me through the window. But it's not shining through the branches of Mrs. Dickerson's elm tree. There's no cricket band sawing away. There's no Karl holding me. There's no one to kiss.

I feel very alone.

Dear Diary,

He was an old man with a long white beard. Not Heidi's grandfather—somehow I knew it was my mother's father, my grandfather. He was standing in a field. Alone, in Russia. Big men in boots ... Cossacks ... were stamping out to him, were knocking him down, stealing his land. That's the scary picture I woke up with this morning.

Does that mean I'll never be able to have my old dream back? The one of my grandfather and me safe on our mountain in Switzterland?

I couldn't help reaching out to the table by my bed and opening *America, The Melting Pot Of The World.* The first page shows the Statue of Liberty with the words, "Give me your tired, your poor, your huddled masses yearning to breathe free." The second page has sad-faced immigrants coming through Ellis Island after World War One, the women and little girls wrapped in shawls, and all seeming to be in a daze as they stared out at the camera. It says they were herded together, poked and inspected, and asked a lot of questions. And they didn't even know a word of English. I caught myself searching for Mom and Dad in the crowd.

Dear Diary,

In the kitchen, just as if nothing awful was said yesterday, my aunt poured me a glass of fresh-squeezed orange juice and told me she thought of something fun for me to do while I'm here. I could be in charge of the socks and handkerchiefs at their store. (Help!!) I was saved by Grace who walked into the kitchen saying that she wanted to take me to her art class today.

I almost bowled my cousin over with my thank you hug.

We took a clanging streetcar to downtown Milwaukee, then walked a block and up some steps into an old gray stone building, where, inside,

I breathed in the strong smells of paint and turpentine. A tall, paunchy, white-haired man, with a big nose and wearing a paint-spattered shirt, came toward us, and Grace introduced me to her teacher, Mr. Ritterband. The teacher smiled, looked me straight in the eye, shook my hand, and said, "Welcome to the community of art." (Gee!) Then Mr. Ritterband led us into an equally paint-spattered room. Grace whispered to me that he's very serious about art, he likes to lecture but he's very nice, and he wants all his students to call him Pop.

Mr. Pop Ritterband set me up on a wooden bench, gave me a slanted board to draw on, a big tablet of newsprint paper and some sticks of charcoal, and announced that the Drawing from Life class was about to begin.

I sneaked looks at the other students. About twelve of us, all ages, straddled benches and faced a platform in the middle of the room. It was so, so still, you could hear a feather fall. Just as I was wondering what was going on, what it was we were waiting for, an old lady in a ratty bathrobe came in from a side door and stepped onto the platform.

And, before I knew what she was doing, before I could look away, she let the robe fall to her feet! My face burned. She was completely naked! And there were people of the opposite sex in the class!

Grace was busily drawing the woman's flabby figure. The man next to me was sketching away as if looking intently at naked old ladies was perfectly normal. I tried drawing her face. Though it was hard not to notice the saggy breasts, the wrinkly nipples, the stomach hanging down in rolls and the bunch of bushy stuff farther down. I thought of sketching the other people in the class, but I was afraid it might be against the rules.

Pop walked around the room, quietly saying a few words to one or another student. When he stopped by me I froze, but he just gave me a pat on the shoulder. After he moved on, a pretty blond-haired girl across the room smiled at me, then made a face at the old lady behind her hand. I could tell she felt the same way about drawing her as I did.

Finally—an eternity later—the old lady pulled on her bathrobe and lit a cigarette, and the rest of us filed out of the room. The pretty girl bought a bottle of Coca-Cola from the machine in the hall. I revived myself by buying a Coke, too.

I just slipped off my nightgown and studied my body in the full-length mirror. What would Karl think if I sent him a drawing of me with bare breasts and everything else? What an insane thought! Never in a million years would I send him that kind of drawing.

Dear Diary,

There's been a new development. Cousin Grace isn't feeling well because of the baby, so she wants me to take her place for the rest of the art-survey course. Starting today!

"Don't be silly, Janet," Grace said to me. (She noticed I wasn't leaping for joy.) "This is a great chance for you to develop your talent. I saw your sketchbook, remember? I know you love to draw."

This means I won't be going home. I won't be seeing my friends . . . or Karl! . . . for three more weeks! I had to agree about taking her place at the art school because I know Grace is doing me a favor. And maybe just a little bit because I really do love to draw. But mostly because it will help give me something different to think about, something other than Jews and Russians and Pogroms.

Dear Diary,

I'm writing this in bed after my first day alone at art school. The school has cost Uncle Abe $32, at least ten dresses worth. I hope it's worth it. And I did feel very grownup taking the streetcar to downtown Milwaukee by myself. But then, in the Drawing from (horrors)

Life Class I erased the old lady so much, all I had at the end of the class were jagged holes in the paper.

In free period I started out to do a serious picture about the war like most everyone else (war-torn landscapes) but my mind wouldn't let me do it, my drawing turned into a crew-cutted boy and a girl in a canoe. I thought of drawing ragged refugees staring up at the Statue of Liberty but the boy and girl showed up again. This time they were on an island on a lake, smooching under an aspen tree and surrounded by lilies of the valley.

At lunch time, I took Aunt Pearl's paper bag lunch out to the courtyard and sat with two girls—Nancy Harcourt, who is eighteen, and Connie Miller, the pretty girl who smiled at me yesterday. Connie is twenty, a college girl, very sophisticated. She's even been to New York City and has seen the Atlantic Ocean. And her waist is so small she can probably eat whatever she wants.

Connie shared her pink-frosted cupcake with me and told me she planned to be a fashion designer; she's good at copying the models in fashion magazines. I'm good at copying magazine pictures; maybe I should become a fashion designer, too.

Goodnight, Dear Diary. It might not be too bad staying here longer. As long as I can keep from being a captive audience for Aunt Pearl.

But I better hear from Karl soon!

Dear Diary,

News from home. Letters and a clipping Mom sent me from the Elksburg Press.

"Janet Kessler, Elksburg High School student, is spending the month of July studying art at the Museum Art School in Milwaukee."

What the notice left out was that Mrs. Kessler was glad to be rid of her ungrateful daughter.

Dad sent me a bunch of letters from servicemen that I'll have to make time to answer. Inside the package was a note from him saying that I should please know that "your mother, my dearest Janet, only wants the best for you."

Poor Mom. All that nagging and screaming. All that silent treatment. Maybe she is trying to do the best for me, but it's never in the right way. I'll try to understand her better from now on.

Here's what I got from Elaine:

Dear Janet,

I heard you're going to art school. Hope you're having a swell time and learning a lot. It's pretty boring here in town except that I'm helping the Overseas War Relief collect old clothes and a bunch of us are knitting more of those khaki colored scarves for our soldiers. My mom and I used up all of our butter ration stamps making fudge to send overseas. Next week I have to go to Methodist Church Camp near New Berlin. My mom wants me to be "saved."

I miss you.

Love from your friend, Elaine

Here's Mary Lou's letter:

Dear Cutie Pie,

Swell news about you and Karl Kunkel!! I've been dating a guy from Deersville, he's 4-F, can't join up 'cause he's got flat feet. Lucky me. We have good necking sessions, but I won't let him go too far. I heard about a girl from around here who got knocked-up by her boyfriend. He took off and now she's going to have a baby at age 16 and her life is ruined. Boy, is that a good lesson for me! I can hardly wait till you come home and give us the scoop on all your adventures in the big city.

Love and kisses from your confidante,
Mary Lou

P.S.1 I ran into Karl outside the feed store. I gave him your address and told him you wouldn't be home for awhile and he said to say hi to you.
P.S.2 New report. I bought more of that dark maroon, guaranteed-not-to-come-off lipstick along with dark maroon nail polish and a new kind of black mascara.
P.S.3 Which reminds me, have you met any cute boys?

For God's sake, Mary Lou, why didn't you write more about Karl? How did he look? Did he seem disppointed that I'd be here longer? How do you think he meant it when he told you to say hi to me?

Dear Karl,
This week I got letters from Marines on some secret Pacific islands, from a soldier in Algeria, a soldier in Italy and a sailor in Australia. And you, Karl? Have you fallen off the surface of the earth?

Of course, I won't send him this letter. In fact I'm not going to write to him till he writes to me. But Karl, why haven't you written? Are you kissing some other girl, holding her close at the dance hall, canoeing with her on the lake? Paddling into the inlet? The two of you finding my secret island?!

Dear Diary,
I'm in bed, as always my favorite place to curl up with you. I'm sorry I haven't written to you the last few days. I'm kept very busy at art school. I'm nearly going nuts with Perspective. I know I'll never understand it. When our class went outside to learn perspective by

drawing the downtown buildings I gave up fast and drew some people on the street instead.

Also, Pop Ritterband is getting me nervous. We've had the same model so many times in Life Drawing I've felt like screaming. And he expects me to concentrate. I know I'd do better if the old lady had a bathing suit on. And in Still Life class where we're painting fruits and vegetables, I chose a cantaloupe because it looked easier. Pop cut it open and is making me paint the insides.

Almost as bad as all that, in free period yesterday we were asked to design War Bond Posters, but my drawing of a refugee with a shawl pulled low over her head and PLEASE! BUY MORE WAR BONDS TO SAVE US! in a balloon coming out of her mouth, still looked less like a refugee and more like Ginger Rogers.

It was a relief today when Pop let us rest by giving us a lecture. "Art has always been with us," he said. "From the days of the caveman all the way up to our modern times." On a big screen, he showed us paintings by artists through the ages. I made notes and will look them up in Grace's art books. Leonardo Da Vinci, Rembrandt, Goya, and Picasso.

I especially liked the portraits by an artist named Vincent Van Gogh. Which made me realize that most of my drawings are portraits, not only of Karl and me, but of Pop Ritterband and the other students in the class as well as people I see on the street.

After the interesting lecture, Pop told us to draw our own portraits. Self portraits, he called them. "Observe the basic structure of your face. Try to capture your "unique essence."

I just looked up unique and essence in Grace's dictionary:

> **Unique**: one and only, having no like or equal,
> highly unusual, extraordinary, rare, etc.

Essence: fundamental nature, important quality (of something) essential being, a flavor or fragrance of a plant, food, etc. Inward nature of anything.

Hmm. the first thing I thought of both as essence and unique were the lilies of the valley on my island. Then, of course, the important and essential quality of kissing. As for people, I guess it's also true that each of us is unique. But aren't all people also supposed to be equal?

Well, to get back to the class, instead of doing a picture of myself, I worked a long time on a portrait of Connie Miller, showed her naturally curly (I think) blond hair, light blue eyes and dark curled eyelashes; made it as pretty as I could, and signed it, "With love and admiration, from Janet." I feel lucky that she, a college girl, is so friendly with a mere not-yet-sixteen-year-old like me. (I lied, told Connie I'm almost seventeen.)

Connie and I giggle in class a lot. We exchanged addresses and I think she's going to become one of my best friends. She even loves Frank Sinatra as much as I do, especially him singing "I'll Be Seeing You." Connie also told me she's only going to art school because her grandmother, who has lots of money, is making her.

"Me too," I told her. Which isn't exactly true since we know I don't have a grandmother. Anyway, I'm beginning to think that I really would like to learn how to do important pictures, like some of the adults in the class are doing. Pictures of nurses on the battlefield saving wounded soldier's lives, things like that.

Connie also confided in me about her fantastically wonderful boyfriend. "He's in the Navy now but he was a sports star, he's still keeping his white convertible, and he's even more gorgeous than Tyrone Power." So I confided in her how I love Karl, how we finally got together on the very last day before I left Elksburg.

Connie is happy for me. She invited me to go to the show with her tomorrow night. I asked her if we could see *Gone With The Wind*.

"Are you kidding?" Connie laughed. *Gone With The Wind* came out a few years ago. It's not playing anywhere, anymore."

Oh, no. It never came anywhere near Elksburg.

P.S. I kind of wish I had brought along my hair curlers. And had some kind of eyelash curler, too.

Dear Diary,

Connie and I went to the show. *The March Of Time* newsreel showed mobs of men with Swastika signs on their sleeves, holding their arms straight out and screaming, Heil Hitler, and I wanted to cover my ears, but with Connie beside me, I managed to keep munching my popcorn. At last we saw hundreds of our planes bombing Germany. "Allies on the offensive," it said. and Connie and I, along with the whole audience, clapped our hands and cheered.

The movie was *Casablanca*. I nearly died near the end when Humphrey Bogart raised his glass of champagne to Ingrid Bergman and said, "Here's looking at you, kid." I died even more at the very end when Humphrey sent Ingrid away, which meant that Ingrid had to sacrifice her true love for a larger cause—freedom and winning the war—and say farewell forever to Humphrey. I would never have the courage to give up a true love like that. I sobbed so terribly as Ingrid Bergman walked off into the mist, I was completely worn out.

Connie was still laughing at me as we sat ourselves in a booth in a Walgreen's Drug Store. She told me my face was all puffy, and did I always cry in movies like that? Her sorority sisters would get a big kick out of me, she said. She even told me I'm cute and have a cute personality and that I'll probably get rushed by lots of sororities. But wherever I go to college, I should definitely join her sorority, Gamma

Something Gamma. I think that's the name she said.

Connie told me that sororities are the greatest part of college. You make your best friends there, you stick together through thick and thin your whole life, you get the neatest men so you have the cutest children, and you all go to the same churches.

Lying here under Aunt Pearl's silky cover, I'm thinking about what she said. Maybe I will join a church someday. A nice one full of beautiful people like Connie. I could do it. It's a free country, I don't have be Jewish, I could be part of the majority. And I always did like "Silent Night" and "Come All Ye Faithful," and Mary Lou's Midnight Mass and Easter Sunrise and her Holy Mother and golden angels that I always draw after I go to church with her.

And to sit and pray along with everyone else. I can see myself with a cross around my neck, not too big, maybe on a thin silver chain.

P.S. I don't know what church Karl belongs to.

P.S.2 If Connie knew I'm Jewish, would she still like me?

Dear Diary,

Cousin Grace has to spend lots of time resting; doctor's orders. I know she misses her soldier husband (he wears glasses so he's not in any danger, being a finance officer in England) so when I'm back at Aunt Pearl's, I sit with her.

Today Grace held out a globe of the world to me, twirled it, and I saw mostly flashes of blue oceans. Then she stopped it and pointed to a big stretch of Europe. "Can you believe it?" she said. "The Nazis conquered all this by 1940. And here." She pointed to Poland and a country I never heard of, called Lithuania. "Both Poland and Lithuania fell in 1941." She looked at me. "It's a terrible, terrible thing that's happening over there."

I nodded, though I didn't exactly know what she meant. To change the subject I turned the globe to see where we were. In the whole of the United States we found a small looking Wisconsin. And in her Atlas, on a big map of just our state, Elksburg was only the teeniest of letters. It seemed very strange.

After that, for some unfathomable reason, Grace insisted on playing a very depressing record for me. "Strange Fruit." "It's about how they hung Negroes in the South on trees," Grace explained to me. "It's called lynching."

"I heard about lynching, Grace." Does she think I don't know anything?

"The Ku Klux Klan still lynches people," Grace kept on. "In fact, we have the Ku Klux Klan wearing white hoods and carrying burning crosses right here in Wisconsin."

Right here? Black bodies hanging from the poplar trees . . .

Unfortunately, Grace noticed me shiver. "Frankly, Janet," she frowned at me, "I don't think they teach you enough in your backwater town."

Backwater town? Well, I wanted to say, "We may only have three thousand people, counting all the farmers who come in to shop, but we have a movie house, a bowling alley, a city hall clock that chimes every hour and, right through town, we have the Elk River. Cornfields and cows are just two blocks from my house and only five miles away is Eagle Lake with canoes and a dance hall, and I even have my own secret island. And along with my friends and the quiet streets at night and the crickets and fireflies and the moon so bright and stars so thick over us, you know almost everybody and almost everybody knows you, and you do not pass a person without saying hello, especially me."

But I didn't argue with Grace. I've even decided to forgive her for lecturing and trying to educate me. After all, she's going to have a baby and she's my only cousin in the world. Most of all, I forgive her because her husband, whom she loves, is far away. Which I think I know how that feels.

Dear Diary,

On the way to art school today I decided to give myself a lecture. Way better than the lecture Grace gave me.

I told myself that I have nothing to be really very sad about. I'm lucky that I live in the good old USA; everyone in the world must wish they were here. We're winning the war and I'm very, very lucky in every other way, too . . . almost. I'm lucky just to be alive. Especially lucky when you think of Hitler, and the war over there, and the Ku Klux Klan and all those poor refugees we collect old clothes for.

But then a deformed woman, an actual dwarf, climbed (with help) onto the jam-packed streetcar and wedged in next to me. My first time I was ever close up to a dwarf. I sneaked a look at her big, square face sitting on top of her short lumpy body, at her long arms and big man's hands, and at her black skirt that reached to her clumpy black shoes. How unlucky can you get? It wasn't her fault she was born like that. I stewed about it through seven stops before I realized there's another reason I'm lucky. I, at least, look normal.

To make a long story short, just before I had to brush past her to get off the streetcar, I made myself smile at her. Her stoney face seemed to crack open; her smile back at me felt like the sun was bursting through. It almost made me forget how she looked.

And I had this thought, that no matter how tall or short or fat or skinny or different we are, we're all human beings. We all have the same human bodies underneath our clothes. We all have behinds, we all have to go to the bathroom. We all have belly buttons from being born.

In free period I drew the lady dwarf, tried to show that the outside of someone doesn't always match what she's like inside. Connie glanced at the portrait, and tittered, and Nancy joined in. I wondered, did my drawing really look goofy?

Before I could turn to the next clean page, Pop Ritterband stopped, patted me on the shoulder and told me that my drawing was a definite improvement. "It shows a sympathetic expression of humanity," was what he said. Back here at home, I looked it up:

> **Humanity**: 1. The fact or quality of being human
> 2. The fact or quality of being humane; kindness, mercy, sympathy, etc.

I love the word, HUMANITY. It makes me think of how I always want everyone to be connected with each other, like on Memorial Day and the Fourth of July when we're marching and showing ourselves and making the music rise up and everyone on the street is cheering us on. Like when I was small and thought I was connected to birds and flowers and every living thing. Like I felt connected to that dwarf lady when she smiled back at me.

P.S. I just realized that I haven't thought about Karl all day.

P.S.2 I wish Connie hadn't said that my drawing looked goofy.

P.S.3 Why do there have to be wars, anyway? Why can't we all just be equal and get along and and have our closed faces crack open when we smile at each other?

Dear Diary,

Today Pop showed us more pictures of animals and humans drawn on the walls of caves. "Prehistoric painters did this powerful work," he said, "often with their bare hands, or with sticks dipped in soil and blood."

Connie poked me. "Soil and blood." For some reason that made her and Nancy break out in giggles. It was a huge effort but I managed to keep my mouth shut and my eyes on Pop.

"Being human means making art, people." (His exact words; he talked slowly and I took notes.) "Thousands of years ago, cavemen lived in a dark and dangerous world. The cave-man artist was considered a kind of magician. By painting images of their lives, the artist-magician helped his clan gain control over their world, made them feel less confused, less afraid of wild animals, less afraid of the elements, like thunder and lightning and eclipses of the moon. Less helpless. That caveman painter made himself feel less confused, less afraid, less helpless."

That's when I got that funny sensation in my chest.

Pop stepped closer and gazed intently at us.

"By making his mark," he said, "by creating his images, the prehistoric artist was saying, I am human. I exist. This is who I am."

Who am I, really?

Dear Diary,

I want to remember this date, July 25, 1943, because I woke up exhausted. But it was a happy exhaustion. I've never had such a wonderful dream before. It started out with deafening thunder, lightning, and black clouds rolling through the sky. Then, suddenly, just like in a movie show, the clouds parted and along with the light, out poured a shiny new band together with hundreds of other people. Drums boomed, clarinets trilled, trumpets blasted out "Stars and Stripes Forever."

A caveman was marching, and soldiers and sailors, and Van Gogh and Rembrandt, and the dwarf lady on the streetcar. A boy who looked like Dad appeared, and then a girl who looked like Mom. Helen Keller was there with her face lifted up, as well as paint-spattered Pop Ritterband. Mrs. Dickenson carried an apple pie. And I was there, laughing, and waving scarves at everyone, not dull khaki scarves, but scarves in every beautiful color. An old man with a white beard—was it my grandfather?—reached down and grabbed my hand and I held on and marched and danced and sang together with everyone else. And still the dream wasn't over; there was so much more . . . more and more faces . . . to see—to draw . . . such amazement.

I want to tell Pop that I think I understand what he said about the cavemen and being human. I want to tell him that I want my drawings to show the good and true humanity of people.

I may not know who I am but I'm pretty sure about that.

Dear Diary,

Before I tell you about my blind date, I have to say that my happy-all-together dream has stayed alive and strong in front of my eyes. Yesterday, when Pop Ritterband brought in a real-life skeleton for us to draw, I couldn't help taking hold of its boney hand and looking into its hollow eyes. Couldn't help thinking that here was once an alive person. Maybe even an amazed person.

Anyway! just as I was beginning to learn about more painters and sculptors in Grace's books, just as I was spending more and more time with my sketchbooks, something else popped up. Remember the soldier Aunt Pearl wanted to fix me up with when I first arrived? Well, he came here to be with his relatives for a few days. This morning I heard my aunt on the phone. "Yes, my lovely niece will be glad to go out with Rudi. The poor boy has agreed? What? Tonight? Oh yes, that's fine. Yes, I know. He needs something normal in his life . . . a nice girl . . . yes."

The poor boy has agreed? He needs something normal? What kind of blind date have I agreed to go out with?

It seems that I was supposed to make a big impression. Grace loaned me her panty-girdle and nylons, and Aunt Pearl gave a new pair of red pumps. I was all spiffed-up and ready in my aqua, princess-style dress when the doorbell rang.

Well, he's eighteen. The same age as Karl. He's not as tall or as good-looking as Karl, but I couldn't help but notice that his shoulders are broad, his eyes are blue, but darker than Karl's, and his hair is blond, a darker blond than Karl's, and curly. He's Rudi Weiss, Private First Class, and in two days he's going back to the army camp. After more basic training he'll learn to be a German language interpreter. That's because he's from Germany, an actual refugee from Hitler.

After he introduced himself and helped me into his uncle's car, he just sat there and stared at me. "You speak English very well," I said for something to say.

He told me he's been here in this country over a year now. "Also, in Germany," he said, "we were taught English in school. That was before some of us were not allowed to go to school."

"Oh." I looked at him sideways. The Nazis.

He started the car and asked me what I'd like to do. I said I didn't know (I would if he were Karl) so we rode all over Milwaukee and ended up at a drive-in movie. In the middle of staring up at Ginger Rogers and Fred Astaire swaying romantically on the big screen, I felt Rudi looking at me. And the next thing I knew, he had grabbed hold of my hand.

And squeezed it. And held on very tight. I didn't know what to do. I only knew that I couldn't hurt his feelings and pull my hand away. And when he asked if he could see me tomorrow night, I said yes.

I just thought—where was Karl in my amazing dream?

Dear Diary,

Another strange and sad night. This time he brought me a powerfully sweet-smelling gardenia. (I love gardenias.) We drove around again and parked by Lake Michigan. A glowing half moon was rising up over the water. I held the gardenia to my nose.

Suddenly, some night bird—an owl, I think—flapped up from the shore. It looked like it was flying to the moon. I said, "Isn't the moon beautiful?" and Rudi blurted, "I wish I could fly up so high. I wish I could escape from this horrible world."

I turned and stared at him. After a minute, he reached into his pocket, took out his wallet, and handed me a photograph. The little girl in the picture had a round face, darkish-blondish braids, and a kind of serious look.

"Oh," I said. "Who is she?"

"My little sister," he said. "Here she is eleven years old. She would be about your age now."

I told him I thought she was very cute. He didn't answer, just kept looking up at the moon. After what seemed an eternity he spoke up. "My sister made up a song about the moon," he said. "Something about being just one small person down here on earth, but that the moon sees her and is her friend. About the moon always protecting her."

Was it her dark eyes looking out at me? Was it because she loves the moon? I felt as if I already knew her. "She's really very cute," I repeated. "What's your sister's name?"

He just kept touching the picture. "I must tell you, Janet. You . . . your smile reminds me of my sister."

"Oh, I think she's much prettier than I am. Rudi," I repeated, "what's your sister's name?"

He didn't answer. Tears spilled out of his eyes and down his cheeks. I've never been with a boy who cried before.

"What's the matter?"

He just shook his head.

My own eyes filled up.

The moon rose higher and smaller. It made a path of shimmery light on the water. And we just sat there with the picture of his little sister.

Finally, Rudi put the picture back in his wallet. And then, again without warning, he threw his arms around me.

He hugged me so hard, so desperately, it scared me a little. But I could feel his heart beating, could feel his sadness. I couldn't help it. I hugged him back.

This page is getting wet with my tears. Because we just sat there with the moon shining down on us and both of us crying and hugging each other and I didn't even know why.

Dear Diary,

This morning Aunt Pearl told me her friend called and said that Rudi left for his army post. I kept my eyes on my orange juice.

She asked me if Rudi and I had a nice time last night. I said "Yes," and kept my head down.

I could feel my aunt looking at me.

"He can't seem to talk with his relatives," she said.

I had to ask. "Talk about what?"

"He didn't tell you? We thought he might be able to confide in someone near his own age. After what he's been through."

"He didn't say anything about that."

Aunt Pearl bit her lip. "Your Uncle Abe doesn't like me to mention it."

"I want to know what it is."

"Janet, I'm sorry I said anything."

"You have to tell me!"

"Maybe another time."

"I have to know!"

"All right, Janet." She took my hand. "Maybe it is something you should know. First it was his parents. Gone. Taken away by the Nazis. We haven't heard what happened to them. Rudi and his sister went into hiding. He was fifteen, she was twelve."

She stopped, looked at me.

I tugged hard on her arm. "I have to know!"

My aunt sighed. "A year later, his sister disappeared."

"Disappeared?"

"We don't know how. She was probably out hunting for food. We think Rudi feels guilty. He was in charge. Later, he joined the underground, was smuggled out . . ."

That minute Uncle Abe walked into the kitchen. His arms were filled with paper bags. He pulled out bagels, salami, lox, cream cheese, pickles, sponge cake, and apple strudel.

"For my favorite niece," he said, and pinched my cheek.

I looked at my aunt. She shook her head and looked away.

It's after midnight. I keep seeing that picture of Rudi's sister. Keep seeing him crying, keep smelling his gardenia. Keep seeing both of us holding each other, my tears mixed in with his. I still can't believe that a person can disappear like that. Just because . . . because she was born who she was.

Oh, my poor old Dear Diary,

I don't want to. I hardly know how to tell you. But I have to. Besides, who else can I tell?

In Life Class I couldn't help doodling Rudi escaping to the moon, Rudi inside the moon, his little sister in the moon. At breaktime I was on the toilet in the lady's room when Connie and Nancy swept in. I kept quiet so they wouldn't know it was me in the stall; I'm always embarassed to have anyone hear me pee.

Connie asked Nancy if she'd joined a sorority yet, and Nancy answered that she hasn't decided which one but that she's already been asked to lots of pledge parties. Connie said, "Good for you," and Nancy laughed and said that one of the parties was really ridiculous. She got this pretty-as-you-please invitation, she said, and she went to the sorority house with complete innocence.

"If I'd known they were Jews . . ."

What? My ears burned.

"I wouldn't have drunk the tea in their pretty little tea cups or have bitten into their pretty little pink-frosted cupcakes. To top it off, they asked me to come back!"

I felt my face flame up.

"My friends are still calling me Miss Jewstein!" Nancy snorted. "Every time we see a Jew we could just die laughing."

"How embarrassing." Connie was laughing, too. "Especially since it's usually the other way around; dirty Jews always trying to get into our sororities!"

I was suffocating, couldn't breathe. I was frozen. I was burning up. I was stuck, frozen to the toilet seat.

They were still laughing when they finally left.

I splashed cold water over my red-hot face for at least five minutes. Then I walked out and tried to act like nothing was wrong.

It didn't work. I told Pop I had a stomachache, ran out of the building, and took the streetcar home.

Dear Diary,

It's after 4:00 a.m. I just whipped off my nightgown and soaped up in the upstairs shower; scrubbed my arms and legs, my breasts, my belly, my private parts, dug into my scalp. I felt my skull, the bones around the hollows of my eye sockets, my cheekbones, my jaw. I rubbed my skin till it hurt.

I stood in front of the full-length mirror and stared at my naked body. It's not any different from yesterday, no different from Connie's, except fatter. We both have the same kind of bones, same kind of insides. We're both skeletons under our skin.

Once Elaine had come over, we were around nine, and she asked me if I was adopted. I'd already been through all that and I said, "Why do people always say that?"

And she said she didn't know, her mother asked her to ask me. "It must be because you're blond and your folks are dark."

"My dad is bald and I'm only blondish."

"Well," she answered, "I think it's because your folks have accents."

"They do not!" I said hotly.

Elaine had seemed uncomfortable. "Well, you know," she said, "I don't care if you're adopted or not."

For the first time I see my mother in me. In the shape of my face, in the space between my nose and mouth, in the shape of my mouth. I see my dad's nose in my face, my dad in that old picture we have at home, the one of him in his German Army uniform.

A towel is wrapped around my wet head. No, it doesn't look right.

I found a long scarf in a drawer, pulled it low over my forehead, and tied it under my chin. The lamplight is falling on my face. The shadows are dark around me.

With a stick of charcoal I sketched my face and body, then smeared the drawing. I carved out my cheekbones and my eyes with a kneaded eraser. I rubbed more and more charcoal into the paper. Till there was just a shadowed face and staring eyes. Till my hands were covered in black.

It's just a nude girl I've been drawing. Just a drawing of an ordinary, small town girl.

No. It's a drawing of a naked refugee. A drawing of someone who's afraid, someone who has to run away from people trying to harm her.

Dear, Dear Friend Diary,

This morning Aunt Pearl called up the stairs. "Janet dear, it's late! Your orange juice is ready!"

I'll tell her I don't feel well, tell her I'm really sick. I can't face them. I can't! But I can't be a coward, either. Today is the last day of art school. I have to say goodbye to Pop Ritterband.

I forced myself to get out of bed. Forced myself to get dressed and go downstairs. Drink my juice. Made myself take the streetcar downtown.

I pretended to be sorting out my drawings when Connie sidled over and said that I seemed so different from my usual happy self today and why was I so quiet, and was anything wrong. I squeezed my eyes shut, grit my teeth, and kept my head down. She asked if it was about Karl. I shook my head. "Well," she said, "maybe later I can give you some more information about men."

How could it be? She was the same cheery girl who laughed when we both got the curse at the same time last week and we had to send Nancy out to buy us some Kotex sanitary napkins.

"Janet." She was whispering in my ear. "I don't think I should wait. I've got to tell you one very important thing now. You've got to know about rubbers. You have to insist that Karl has rubbers with him, and that he knows how to use them. I'd feel awful if you . . . ."

I was saved by Pop Ritterband coming toward me; it was my turn for a final critique. Connie had to retreat.

Pop sat down on my bench. He glanced at my pile of sketchbooks, pulled out my last one and turned the pages.

I held my breath.

He stopped at the drawing of me with the scarf on my head.

He looked at me. He looked back at the drawing. He said, "There is real feeling here, Janet."

Did it show that much? But what did he see?

The fear?

Or the numbness.

"Do you know what you've done here? How you made the form come out of the shadows? How you used lights and darks to create what you wanted to express? Is there anything you want to tell me about your drawing?

I shook my head.

May I show it to the rest of the class?"

"No. Please."

"All right. But I want you to know that you have something to say, Janet." He put his arm around me. "About humanity," he said. "About our times. And that you're beginning to say it."

I thanked him. Then I packed up my stuff and walked as steadily as I could—I didn't look to my right or my left—out of the gray stone art school building. Out into the air. Out into the sunshine. Out onto the plain old everyday-business street wih everyday people hurrying past each other. Why didn't I ever tell Connie I was Jewish? Why didn't I confront them today? Why didn't I slap both their faces!

I caught a glimpse of myself in a department store window. Superimposed on a naked, perfectly formed mannequin with a tiny waist.

Dear Diary,

It's Sunday, August 1. Tonight Uncle Abe turned on the radio and we sat around the living room listening to President Roosevelt's Sunday night fireside chat.

"My fellow Americans. We hail our victory over Mussolini, we celebrate his fall. As for Hitler and Hirohito, the remaining Axis powers, there will be no escape for them, no safe place for them, no asylum."

I went outside. The night was full of shadows. I stood on the sidewalk, looked back into my uncle's big lighted window, then back into the darkness.

Dear Diary, I want to escape to my safe place, my asylum.

Dear Friend Diary, I want to go home.

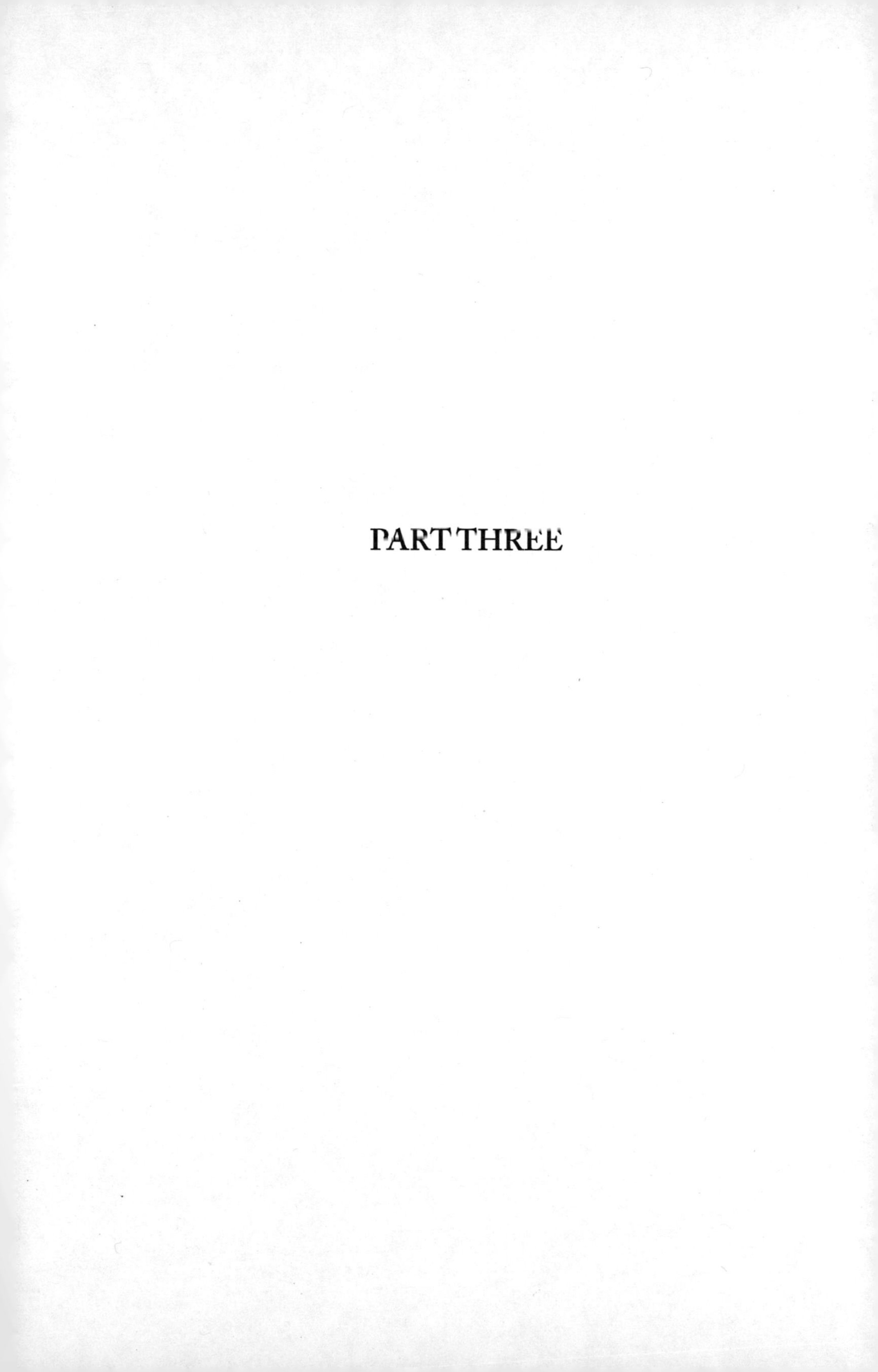

PART THREE

Dear Diary,

I'm writing this on the train. Aunt Pearl didn't ask me any questions before I got on the streamliner, maybe she noticed my red eyes. Besides my own small suitcase and knapsack, I left with a big case loaded with presents: a set of watercolors and two sketchbooks from Grace and Aunt Pearl, a slack suit from Uncle Abe, and a huge Hebrew National salami, two jars of herring in sour cream, three Jewish rye breads, two dozen bagels, four boxes of matzo and two bottles of Maneschewitz wine. Plus "to give you strength for the four hour trip," my uncle slipped me a corned beef on rye sandwich wrapped in wax paper.

"Food like this you don't get up north," he said. "Your mother, she should never have moved so far. Tell her I said so."

At every town going north, servicemen from bases near Milwaukee and Chicago are getting off the train, and girlfriends, mothers, fathers, and grandparents are dashing up to them. I'm sitting with my forehead pressed against the window staring at all the people—at all their different sizes and shapes; at the different angles of their cheeks and foreheads; at their noses, mouths, and ears; at the faces of all these people. Do any of the alone ones, and the not-alone ones, the smiling ones and the not-smiling ones, do their faces cover up what they're feeling inside like mine probably does?

In the crowd, giggling with their heads together, are two girls about eleven or twelve years old. When I was twelve, I got my second new bike; I'd left my first one out in the snow and it got ruined. When I was twelve, I snuck down to Loreen's Beauty Parlor and got my braids cut off and began curling my hair. I had crushes on two boys at the same time.

When Rudi's sister was twelve she disappeared.

The train has lurched to a stop, and a tall Negro soldier has come down the aisle looking for a seat. The man across from me quickly lifted his suitcase onto the empty seat next to him. The soldier stood for a long minute staring down at the man; the man kept his nose in his newspaper. Finally, the soldier slammed down next to me and snapped open his own newspaper.

We're speeding past stretches of corn, taller than a man now, and ready to harvest, past green pastures and almost grown calves, past small towns with their city halls, churches, and Farmer's Feed Co-ops.

A huge sign screamed past:

Believe In Him! He Is Your Savior!
His Blood Was Spilled For Your Sins!

"Ha!" the soldier let out a snort "You see that? In war time we Negroes can die for you, can spill our blood for you, but do you think the Red Cross will mix our blood with yours?" He was almost shouting. "We can't even be buried next to you, for Christ's sake!"

The other passengers clucked their tongues. I huddled down in my seat. Would the soldier laugh in my face if he knew what I was thinking?

That I couldn't be buried next to them, either.

That I'm not white either.

Dear Diary,

I'm home. It's late and my parents are in bed. I tiptoed down the stairs and let myself out the front door. Armies of crickets were sawing away in the quiet night and fireflies began to play tag around me. I stood under Mrs. Dickerson's tree and smelled her delicious roses and new-cut grass. The Milky Way lit up the night.

Earlier, at Appleville station, my dad had rushed over. My mother peered at me. "Are you all right? What is it? Is something wrong?"

"Nothing's wrong, Mom. I'm okay."

She felt my forehead. "You are a little warm."

I wouldn't be surprised if she could see what's inside my head.

"I'm okay, Mom."

They looked at each other. I could almost hear, "little children, little problems, big children, big problems."

"Are you hungry? Mrs. Dickerson has baked chocolate cookies for you."

The chocolately smell filled the car. "No thanks, Mom." I hadn't taken more than two bites of the corned beef sandwich after the Negro soldier got off the train two stops before me.

My room is exactly as I left it. Mrs. Dickerson's elm tree is still trying to get in my window. Ginger Rogers, Frank Sinatra, Clark Gable, and Scarlett O'Hara are still on my wall. Heidi and all of my yearbooks and drawing pads and scrapbooks are still on my shelves, letters and souvenirs from servicemen are still piled on the other twin bed. More shelves still hold every birthday card, every Christmas and Easter card, every Valentine, even the stupid one I got from a boy in fourth grade . . . "Janet is a Big Fat Pig" . . . that's how I knew he liked me. Nothing has been thrown out.

My vanity with its mirror and two drawers, one for pencils, pens, and jewelry, and one for makeup and my metal curlers, is still against one wall. The sketch of Karl Kunkel and the words to "I'll Be Seeing You" are still on my mirror.

I wasn't alone for long; I heard them on the stairs. Mom carried in her "just-made today" chicken soup, felt my forehead again, told me to go to sleep and went back downstairs.

My dad sat down on my bed.

"Well, honey . . . " He seemed almost shy of me.

I gave him a weak smile.

"How was it learning to be an artist? Whoever comes into the store knows how proud of you I am, my artist daughter."

"Oh, Daddy. Please. I'm not an artist yet."

"So different you look. Older. More grown-up. But maybe you would still like to hear a little joke?"

For the first time I was conscious of his foreign accent. I noticed how yellow his fingers were from smoking. The lamplight outlined his sharp nose, his sticking-out cheekbones, his bald skull.

I shook my head.

"You don't want a joke?"

"No, Dad."

He was wearing his funny-sad smile. "Something I have learned, my sweet Janet, always it is better to laugh than to cry."

Why does he always have to say that? It's as bad as his "You're only young once," and "Everything turns out for the best," and "You have your whole life ahead of you."

Down the block, through front-room windows, I saw neighbors sitting around their radios. Across the river, the city hall clock chimed the hour and around the corner, late-night kids were playing kick the can. An owl hooted in Mrs. Dickerson's tree. Someone called out, "Home safe!"

This is where I need to be. Where I know every crack and bump in the sidewalk and where nobody passes a soul without saying hello. Where I will not keep worrying about Rudi Weiss and his sister. Where I will not think about Jews and Hitler and pogroms and the "Strange Fruit" record and that angry Negro soldier on the train. Where I will not keep thinking about hideous Connie Miller and her Gamma something Gamma Gamma.

Where I will forget that picture of Rudi's sister.

I jumped into some faint hopscotch marks on the sidewalk.

Where I'm home. Safe.

Dear Diary,

The morning light is streaming through Mrs. Dickerson's elm tree, is making leafy patterns on Karl on my mirror. Outside, a robin, maybe one of the babies I knew before they were born, is chirping, "Cheer up, cheer-up, cheerup." On the bottom of my suitcase is the 1943 yearbook.

I turned to Karl's picture. To his words.

To a cute kid and a good artist.

Be seeing you around.

But wait, maybe he's been drafted. Maybe he's already in the fighting. Maybe that's why he didn't write to me.

Downstars the phone is ringing. Maybe it's him.

I stood for a minute, composing myself before I answered.

"Welcome home, Janet."

"Oh. Oh, hi, Elaine. Thanks. It's good to be back."

"I've organized a sleep-out in your honor tonight," she said. "Most of our gang can come. We want to hear all about Milwaukee."

"Okay. Thanks. I'll see you later."

The phone again.

"I can hardly wait to see you tonight," Mary Lou bubbled.

"Me, too. Uh, Mary Lou, you haven't seen Karl around, have you?"

"No, I haven't. Did he ever write to you?"

"No." I had to admit it.

"You're not still interested in him, are you?"

"I'm . . . I'm not sure."

"Well, he's still here, you know.

"Oh."

Mary Lou kindly changed the subject. "Elksburg might seem boring to you now."

"Oh, no."

"You haven't changed any, have you? You're still my same old funny friend?"

"Of course."

No. Not quite.

Not quite the same.

Under a pile of newspapers I found last week's Elksburg Press. Under the usual, "Our Boys In The Service" column was a notice.

Our Farm Boys Are Exempted
From Military Service Until Further Notice.
Many Are Disappointed By The Order,
But They Are Still Needed At Home To Help With Our Country's Crucial Food Production

So he's not in the thick of combat. He's not lying bleeding from a fatal bayonet wound. He's not calling out my name.

Karl is still on his farm.

Dear Diary,

It's the middle of the night, I'm writing this by flashlight. I don't feel very well, my head aches, but this whole outing is to welcome me home so here I am in the campground by the woods.

We've stuffed ourselves with the last roasted marshmellows. The fire has settled down into ashes. And I'm surrounded by darkness. Surrounded by my friends' warm, sleeping bodies, my friends I've known my whole life. An enormous sky full of stars is hanging over our invisible dot on the map.

Six of us have biked here to a campground in the woods, cooked our weiners and marshmallows, spread our blankets on the ground, and lay head to head in a circle.

"Tell us about art school," Elaine asked. "What did you learn?"

"Well," I answered, "I learned to draw a naked old lady."

Everyone squealed.

"Will you draw me sometime?" Mary Lou asked.

"But not naked," Elaine said, shocked.

"Did you make any new friends?"

"No, not really."

"Didn't you mention someone in a letter?" Mary Lou asked. "An older girl at art school?"

"That was nothing." My voice came out too loud. "There was nobody."

"Oh." I could tell Mary Lou was puzzled. "Well, did you get a chance to meet any cute boys?"

Yes, I met Rudi who cried. Rudi, who's too sad to talk about.

"I didn't have a chance, Mary Lou. But I did see thousands of servicemen wandering around Milwaukee."

Everyone groaned.

"And here we are," Mary Lou groaned louder. "Way up here in the sticks, and hard up for men."

Except for a farm boy still on the farm.

"Yes," chorused Jean and Joyce. "We're at the worst age for the war. Pretty soon we'll have to share whatever boys are still left."

"Speaking of servicemen," Elaine interjected, "you know that girl from Deersville who got pregnant? My mom heard about another girl like that. Her so-called boyfriend joined the Navy in a big hurry. A fake doctor down in Chicago got rid of her baby for her, but now she has a terrible infection and she might never be able to have children at all."

That shut us up for awhile. Until Mary Lou broke the gloom with a giggle. "Remember when Janet thought you could get pregnant by sitting on a boy's lap? And when we were already in sixth grade Janet still insisted that babies were born through your belly button! She actually informed me that the belly button opened up like a flower and the baby popped out."

My face felt blotchy-hot, but I laughed along with the others.

"And then, when I told her the truth," Mary Lou sputtered so much she could hardly get the words out, "when I told her how babies really are born, she said, well, you may be right, but I still prefer the belly button method."

They all roared.

"Well, I said, "as long as this is confessing time, I'm glad my belly button goes in and not out like the ugly ones, even though stuff does get caught in there."

The others, even Elaine, shrieked, held onto their stomachs and rolled on the ground. Dad would be proud of how I can make my friends laugh.

"And remember?"... they still didn't stop. "Last summer when some older girls said we could be in their club, but only if each of us swallowed a live minnow, and we all rushed to collect minnows in our hats and we were all done and Janet was still gagging and turning purple and the minnow was dead by the time she got it down?"

I remembered. I could still feel the poor, little sticky-dry thing caught in my throat. But would they really not let me into the club if I couldn't swallow the minnow?

I haven't forgotten the Christmas tree. When I was nine, I snuck out at midnight, dragged a leftover fir tree branch home from the tree lot, then leaned it against our front room wall and filled a stocking up with an apple and orange for my surprise on Christmas morning. That was the year my mother gave in. Every Christmas after that a tree sparkling with tinsel stood proudly in our front room window. Just like everybody else's.

"Hey," I practically shouted, "what about the time you all came over to my house and we danced in the front room with only our training bras and underpants on and pretended we didn't know that the boys were outside glued to the window?"

That made everyone whoop so much they ended up wiping their cheeks free of tears. "Help!" shrieked Mary Lou, "I just peed in my pants!"

Elaine calmed down first. "We're going to be juniors in high school, girls. With the way we're behaving it doesn't seem possible."

Everyone agreed. And fell over laughing.

We were quiet for awhile, then someone started singing, "That Old Black Magic." Then it was "It Had To Be You" and "All Or Nothing At All" and "I Don't Want To Set The World On Fire," all at the top of our voices. We sang "This Love Of Mine" and every other Hit Parade song we could think of.

We sang, "I'll Be Seeing You" by Frank Sinatra.

Until Mary Lou piped up. "Remember in first grade? We had to watch out for Janet. She'd have kissing spells and run after everybody trying to hug and kiss them."

I made a quick grab for Mary Lou. "And I haven't changed, either!" Shirley, Jean, and Joyce piled on top of us and we rolled over and over, whooping and shrieking and tickling each other. Even Elaine got into the act. I laughed harder than anyone.

A star just streaked across the sky.
I wish I may, I wish I might, have the wish . . .
So many wishes.
For an end to hatred and ugliness.
For it to be like it was before, when I didn't know anything.
And for love.
No matter what's going on in the world, how much I need love.

Dear Diary,

Daddy said I look pale and should have a little rest after my time in the big city. I've had tons of "good for whatever ails you" chicken soup but I don't feel like drawing or anything else so I just sat in the front room and listened to soap operas on the radio. At night we listened to the news. We're still fighting the Germans in Italy, but they're still in control of Poland. Mom went to bed and Daddy smoked one cigarette after another. I was too tired to stay up for the Hit Parade.

Rudi's gardenia is all withered but, damn it, I can't bear to throw it away.

Dear Diary,

A letter today. I didn't know if I was glad to get it, or not. But here it is. From Rudi.

Dear Janet,

I hope this finds you feeling fine. Thank you for being so understanding last week. You are a special girl to sit with me as you did. I will finish my training in Fort Bliss, Texas. But I am impatient. I want to already be in Europe forcing information out of those Nazi swine.

Remember I showed you the photograph of my sister? I want you to keep it for me until the war is over.

I shook the envelope. The picture fell out. Blondish braids. Round face. Dark eyes. A kind of serious look.

On the back of the photo Rudi wrote:

Dear Janet, Don't forget this girl.
Her name is Lilly.

The funny feeling is in my chest. It's as if this girl named Lilly, who is now as old as I am, could really be as close to me as a sister—as if, if she were here, she could fill up the other twin bed. As if I could tell her my deepest feelings. And her name. She's named after my favorite flower.

I hauled out my sixth grade scrapbook and found a photograph of me. My hair is in braids, I'm wearing a cute sun suit and I'm standing proudly with my new blue bike. I looked closely at Rudi's sister and then at me again. With our dark eyes and round faces we could be twin sisters. We even have the same serious look.

Dear Rudi,

Thanks so much for the picture of your sister. I promise I'll take good care of it. I remember you told me it was taken when she was eleven. I love her name. Was Lilly named for my favorite flower, the lily of the valley? I know you told me she loves the moon. So I guess she likes being outdoors in nature like me. Does she like to draw?

I found a year-old snapshot of me in a canoe—a good one, I look skinny—and enclosed it, then signed my letter with, Love, Janet.

I thought a minute and added a sketch of a tiny child reaching up out of a lily of the valley.

Of course I couldn't tell him what Aunt Pearl told me, that his sister is lost. And I feel bad telling you this, too. But Dad's right. It's better to laugh than to cry. I'm home in Elksburg now and I can't . . . I won't . . . let myself be sad. I'm hiding the picture of Lilly between the pages of my grade scrapbook.

Dear Diary,

I woke up to a million birds in Mrs. Dickerson's tree, then lay in bed listening to all the church bells. No smell of coffee from downstairs. No smell of bacon for me. The folks were already down at the store, Dad with his usual Sunday marking of merchandise, and Mom at her sewing machine keeping up with the alterations.

I got out of bed and poked my nose into the tree. I looked out further, and across the street, at the grade school playground, some little girls were swinging as high as they could go. Below, on the sidewalk, a boy was wobbling on a two-wheel bike with training wheels. Those girls will grow up free and easy without heavy weights hanging over them. The boy's biggest worry in the world is learning how to ride a bike.

I pulled my head back in. After my friends get home from church I'm going to invite them over.

All five of my friends claimed they've been dying for Hebrew National hot dogs, corned beef, Jewish pumpernickel rye bread, bagels, cream cheese, lox, herring in sour cream and kosher dill pickles. "Boy, are you lucky," they kept saying, as they stuffed themselves to the gills.

I drew pictures of everyone and gave each of them their portraits. Mary Lou brought over some of her grandma's butter ration coupons so we made some fudge for dessert.

To top it all off, I jumped up and said I had a great idea. "Let's all hunt up our old roller skates and go skating like we used to."

It took some convincing but, for a change, everyone finally agreed and they went home and dug out their skates. Back at my house we attached our skates to our shoes and tightened them up with our skate keys.

We skated up Main Street which was deserted except for the bars and taverns. We skated past Bob's bowling alley, the Royal Movie House, and the Farmer's Feed Co-op. Past Loreen's Beauty Parlor, past Kessler's Dry-Goods Store, MacDougal's Tap, and Richter's Bar and the men standing outside.

We hogged the sidewalks skating past our neighborhoods and the high school, past the Methodist church, the Congregational church, the Lutheran church, the Catholic church, the Catholic Parish Hall, and poor Mr. Stubenbaker's house, and Mr. Thorpe's house, and Eugene Wilson's house who was crippled in this war. We skated past my house twice; I waved at the kids on the elementary school playground swinging on the swings.

Tonight President Roosevelt's fireside chat told us that the tide of war has turned against the Axis. "But the times are tragic," he told us. "We must still be brave here on the home front and must continue to give our all."

And then the news. "Allied victories in the Pacific. The Russian Red Army overrunning German defenses. Killing and bloodshed all over Europe."

Dad turned off the radio and lit a cigarette.

And stuck in a sketchbook, Rudi's gardenia is all brown and dead.

Dear Diary,

I thought about being on my secret island. Of being alone with the wind and the waves and the egret and the dragonfly, and maybe even a few lilies of the valley might still be hiding under the aspen tree. But I have to confess I was afraid to be by myself. Afraid that I might start thinking too much, might start being sad and mixed up again. So this week I only rode my bike to the lake with my friends. We picnicked and swam and rented canoes, and hooted and laughed and tried to turn each other's canoes over in the middle of the lake.

I just turned back to the page where I wrote about joyfully waving the many colored scarves. The dream I had. It was on July 25.

The night before I met Rudi.

Dear Diary,
Did it really happen? All the good stuff at art school with Pop Ritterband and hearing about the cavemen and Van Gogh, and drawing that picture of the lady dwarf, and learning about the Community of Art? I know it did; it's written down just like I'm writing this now. And the drawing of the lady dwarf is still in my sketchbook. But it's almost like I've turned my back on it all. Like I've tried hard to do with Rudi and his little sister. That girl. Like me. Named Lilly.

No more time. It's Saturday. I'm late. I have to work at the store. Thank goodness, no more time to think.

Dear Diary,
I have a lot to tell you. But first of all I have to start at the beginning. This morning Dad asked me (now that I'm a regular "artist") to get out the roll of white shelving paper, the poster paint, and the ruler and make a new poster for the store.

Notice
The Elksburg Chamber of Commerce has voted
that stores should be open on Saturday night
so that the farmers can do their shopping
before church on Sunday

But not till he made me listen to a joke.

"Two men were talking. Man One said, 'That farmer is a cruel man.' Man Two said, 'What makes you say that?' Man One, 'You see the ears of corn? You see how he's pulling them?'"

I managed a smile and Daddy looked grateful. I got out the paper and paint and in an hour I had the poster made. Dad added the usual signs to the display.

Remember Our Boys In The Service
Alterations Free Of Charge
Buy War Stamps With The $ You Save

And the smaller sign:

The Customer Is Always Right

Main Street was busy. Kids rode up and down in their Tin Lizzies, honking their tinny horns. Farmers and their families still came in for marked-down work clothes, and girls snapped up the on-sale bathing suits. Stuck-up Mrs. Schweiner still managed to mangle the socks and underwear and not buy a one, and I was kept busy helping the Jamaican farm workers pick out gifts to send back home.

It was almost closing time and—oh, God, there he was.

Karl. Outside on the sidewalk. Alone, not with Morrie Fitzgerald. Waving and smiling at me. What should I do? Should I ignore him?

It was like my feet were my brains. Before I could stop myself . . . I barely heard Dad asking me where I was going . . . I dashed out to the sidewalk. Karl led me around the corner and into his pickup truck, and we drove to the A&W Root Beer Stand at the edge of town.

We ordered our drinks and slipped into the back booth. I said, "Thank you for the root beer float." What I wanted to say was, where have you been? Why didn't you call me up? Why didn't you write me a letter?

Instead, like an idiot, I began to babble. Mostly about how good it was to be home again. I even confessed that, though he doesn't look a bit like him, he reminds me a little of Frank Sinatra.

He kept gazing at me and smiling.

"Janet." He finally opened his mouth. "I'm glad you're back. I'm not much good at writing letters. But I did think about you."

Slowly, sitting opposite him, gazing at him, fireworks began to sparkle around his blond head. I felt myself disappear into his electric-blue eyes.

"I've been thinking," he said, "You were at an art school and I really admire your drawing. I can't draw a straight line. D'ya think you could make a picture of me? Right here?"

"Karl, I don't have anything to draw with."

He went to the counter and came back with paper and a pencil.

He gazed at me, posed for me. I tried to concentrate. I could hardly hold on to the pencil.

And then I was getting it—the shape of his head, the set of his ears, the space between his eyes, his delicious lips. It started to really look like him. The only problem was, I couldn't get past his eyes and his smile to what was inside.

All at once I was shaky. I felt my face flare up. My heart thumped.

I blurted, "I'm Jewish."

"I know," he said. He didn't blink an eye; he still had the same smile on his face.

We parked in front of my house and drank some of his Southern Comfort. And oh!—the way he kissed me! I got so worked up I had feelings "down there." But just as Karl slipped his hands under my blouse (oh, God!) the outside light went on and the front door opened. My dad was on the stoop.

I had to leave him. I had to get out of the car.

It's 2:00 a.m. This is it, dear God, or whoever. I can't not have someone to love.

3:00 a.m. Of course he knows I'm Jewish. Everybody does. But I'm still glad I said it. I've never said it out loud before.

Dear Diary,

Before I get to the important part, I have to say that it's been one and half weeks since I heard from Karl. It hasn't been easy to keep my smiley face pasted on. Anyway, to start off, I need to mention that there've been signs all over town for weeks.

Hello Neighbor!!
Hi-Ho! Let's Go!
To The Lake County Fair!
Splendid Exhibits!
County Championship Softball Games!
War And Farm Equipment Displays!

Naturally, Dad said I could get off work and Elaine and I got a ride to the Fairgrounds with Mary Lou and her mother. Mrs. Sweeny went off to try and win the pickle canning contest while we paid the ten cents grandstand admission fee and watched Elaine's uncle and his team of dray horses get second prize—$10—in the horse-pulling contest.

At the baseball diamond, we cheered on Mary Lou's married brother who was pitching for the Elksburg Elks. We kept up our strength by gobbling big chunks of Mrs. Dickerson's apple pie with cheddar cheese at the Women's Christian Service Baked Goods Stand. Then we watched other people stuffing themselves like pigs in the rhubarb pie-eating contest. I was beginning to wish I'd brought a sketchbook,

In the Livestock Exhibit tent—at the Pork For Defense section—we gawked at a porker so big he filled up a whole pen. His tall, beer-bellied owner stood proudly next to a sign: This Champion Blue-Ribbon Pig Is Going To Be The Biggest Fat Producer In The State! My fingers itched to draw a funny picture of the two of them.

Then, rubbing down a pig in the next stall, Oh God!

"Hello, Janet."

Karl's face was sweaty. His overalls were covered with straw.

Instantly, my mother flew into my head. I didn't know whether to laugh or to cry. My mother, the champion despiser of pigs. My mother who gags when she even sees a picture of a pig.

He smiled. His eyes were fixed on mine. My knees felt weak. Of course. He hasn't called me up because he's been busy getting ready for the Fair.

"Wanna go on the Future Farmer's Hayride tonight?"

My voice came out faint. "Okay."

I couldn't think what else to do so I reached out and patted his pig. The beer-bellied farmer next door scowled at me. Did I do something wrong? Elaine grabbed my arm; I just had time to wave goodbye to Karl.

"Your face is beet red, Janet," Elaine said outside the tent. "I guess you've got it bad for Karl Kunkel. My folks know the Kunkels; that old sourpuss is Karl's dad."

Dear Diary,

"Who are you going with?" Mom automatically asked.

"With my girlfriends," I automatically answered.

"Which girlfriends?"

"Oh, you know . . . Elaine." She approves of dependable Elaine.

"And Elaine's uncle"—I got carried away—"Well, his championship team of dray horses are pulling the wagon."

My mother gave me her eagle eye.

I gave her my eagle eye back.

"All right," she said. "But don't be late."

I pulled on my new, rolled-up blue jeans, then spent half an hour trying to decide which blouse to wear. I wish I had some of Mary Lou's guaranteed-not-to-come-off lipstick.

I'll write more when I get back from the hayride.

Dear Diary,

It's the middle of the night. I didn't want to think about it but I can't sleep. But, as always, and because I promised, I'll start at the beginning.

Karl's truck was parked down the block from my house. Which was smart; it was almost as if he knew my mother would disapprove of him.

Ten minutes later, on a bumpy dirt road, twelve of us piled onto a haywagon, Mary Lou and her date up in front, Karl and me in back, half-buried in the straw.

As soon as everyone was settled, the driver snapped his whip, the horses whinnied, and we were on our bumpy, rolling-from-side-to-side way.

Karl's arm was slung around my shoulders; it was like he was announcing to everyone, "This is my girl, this is who I choose." A couple of farm girls snuck looks at us; they were probably wondering how I ever snagged him.

Beyond the cornfields a glowing-orange half-moon rose slowly, majestically, up into the night. Everything—the balmy night, the moon, the whole scene—except for Morrie Fitzgerald who was being obnoxious waving a bottle of Southern Comfort around—was like a beautiful painting, was perfect.

Except that the moon was exactly how it was that night with Rudi.

The moon rose higher and changed to silver. Someone started singing. "By the light . . . of the silvery moon . . . with my honey I'll spoon . . ."

And with the moon, and the song, and with Karl looking so shiny and innocent in the moonlight with straw in his hair, I could almost make myself believe that the time with Rudi never happened. That it wasn't true about Lilly. That the same moon couldn't be looking down on people being killed or hated . . . or disappeared. That there couldn't possibly be anything so terrible in the world.

Someone else started, "Roll me over . . . in the clover . . . roll me over, lay me down and do it again," the bottle of Southern Comfort was passed around and soon all the couples were doing it (I mean necking), Karl and me included. The whole wagonload felt like a jiggly-giggly, slobbery ocean.

And now the bad part. We passed some of the Jamaican farm workers sitting around a campfire, and singing, like us. They smiled and waved at us, I waved back, and Morrie gave me a dirty look. Then he told a stupid joke about Negro people, only he called them niggers.

Some of the kids snickered. Even Karl laughed. I'm sure the workers didn't hear it, but it gave me a bad feeling. Now I'm mad at myself. I should have said something then. I should have said something to Karl afterward. Even though I know he was just trying to humor Morrie because they've grown up together, and are best friends, and Morrie was drunk.

Dear Diary,

I'm sorry I haven't written to you in awhile. The morning after the hayride, I dragged myself and my bedclothes down to the basement. Mom, pink-faced from the steamy wash water, had already rinsed out the Monday morning laundry, and was pushing it through the wringer. It was too late to throw my sheets in the tub.

My mother stared at me with her x-ray eyes. She sniffed at my pillowcase and made a disgusted face

Oh, lordy, I thought. Here we go.

It turned out that she had called up Elaine's mother and found out that Elaine was not on any hayride; Elaine was at home knitting khaki-colored scarves for the soldiers.

And then, "What are you trying to hide? I can't trust you an inch!"

And so on and so on; once she gets going she can't stop. Only this time, I screamed, "Shut up!" and ran out of the basement.

I was glad I had to put the sheets back on my bed. The pillowcase smelled like Karl's hair lotion too, not only Southern Comfort.

Dear Diary,

Dad tried to make peace between us with his usual, "Our daughter, she is young . . . a harmless lie . . . no harm will come . . ." To me, he said that my mother had a hard life when she was young, she worries, she feels there is danger in the world for young girls like me, and that I should please be good and apologize to her.

I forced myself to knock on her bedroom door and say it. "I'm sorry, Mom." All the time thinking that I wouldn't let her catch me again.

Dear Diary

Monday is still do-or-die wash day. My mother still fries bacon along with the eggs some Sunday mornings, still holding her nose. She seems more tired than ever but she's still giving blood. And now, beginning a few days ago, she's even joined Mrs. Dickerson at the Methodist church after work three times a week, rolling bandages for the wounded. Early this morning, Mrs. Dickerson dropped in with an apple pie and cheese, together with a huge bouquet of her red roses. "For your dear mother," she told me as I arranged the flowers in a milk bottle. "Your mother is one of the most Christian people I know."

Dear Diary,

Once I called up Karl but his unfriendly mother answered the phone, said he was working, and hung up before I could leave him a message.

My friends and I still collect kitchen grease, scrap metal, and tin cans to make guns. We still write morale-lifting letters to our guys overseas; we take turns using up butter ration stamps to make fudge for boys in the service (mostly). The Victory Volunteers say they need our help with their old clothes drive again, and the Congregational Church wants us to help with their fundraiser dinner. And my dad keeps turning off the news on the radio whenever I'm around.

Still, more than once, I hear the words "Nazis, starvation, killing." More than once I feel a pang remembering the picture of Lilly, lying face down, in my sixth-grade scrapbook.

Dear Diary,

There's a big sign in the Royal Theatre lobby.

One Old Shovel Equals
Four Hand Grenades!
Tonight your scrap iron is your admission.

Our gang brought parts of old lawn mowers, rusty saws, and broken hammers to get in. We gobbled popcorn and watched movie-star servicemen singing and dancing in *This Is the Army*. They were having such a great time you'd never know there was a real war on.

After the movie we squeezed into a booth in Pischelmeyer's Drug Store and ordered our hot fudge sundaes. It was Elaine's idea to have a contest on which one of us could make our sundae last the longest.

Unfortunately, I slurped the fastest so I slipped a sketchbook out of my knapsack till the others were finished.

After slowpoke Elaine won, she peered at my doodle and asked, "Who's that?"

I looked at what I drew. It was someone with a round face. With braids. With a serious look.

"She looks like you when you had braids, Janet."

"It's nobody."

I quickly turned the page and drew funny portraits of my friends.

Dear Diary,

Not Elaine. Not Mary Lou. For sure, not my parents, gone to do their Sunday catch-up work at the store. If we're ever going to be really close, it's Karl I need to tell. He probably doesn't even know about all the evilness in the world—and I'm not sure he'd understand—but it's Karl I need to confide in about what happened to Lilly.

Someone just rang the doorbell. More later.

It was him! He said he snuck out of church and parked down the street till he saw my folks leave, and could we go up to my room for a quick "session?" I told him no, first I needed to talk to him. About something important. About some terrible things happening in Europe. About a friend, Rudi, and his sister, from Germany. About what the Nazis are doing.

"You mean the war?"

"No, besides the fighting. It's about them doing bad things to . . . to people."

Why couldn't I still say it? Why couldn't I say Jewish people?

"But that's what war is, Janet. Killing the enemy, doing bad things to people. Anyway," he gave me his heart-stopping smile, "all that has nothing to do with us. Let's not talk about it, okay?"

"But . . ."

"We don't really need to talk at all, do we?"

"Yes we do, Karl! We need to . . ."

He reached for me. I melted into puddle. His arms around me were so strong.

"Janet, I can't wait, I want to kiss you so much. Can we go up to your room?"

We fell on my bed. Our lips and bodies pressed together. He lifted my blouse and touched my breasts. I nearly died! I didn't hear her on the stairs.

She flung open my door. Karl jumped up, ran past her, and down the stairs. There was a long frozen moment. Outside, his truck rattled off.

My mother's voice was dead-quiet. "Look at yourself."

I stumbled to the mirror. My hair was matted, my face was blotchy, my lips were puffed up.

Then it came.

"You let someone like that into your bedroom? Do you want to throw your life away? What kind of person is this who runs off like a criminal? Do you know anything about him?"

"Yes!" I fell back on my bed. "And he's not a criminal!"

"Nevermind! How old is this person? Eighteen? Nineteen? He is taking advantage of you! And his family! Does his family know what he's doing?"

"Why should they? He's not doing anything wrong!"

"Don't be so sure! I know about his family."

She'd been talking with Elaine's mother again. I pulled the covers up to my chin. "It's not his fault that his dad raises pigs!" I yelled. "Just like it's not my fault that you and Dad have a store, and we have to kowtow to people we don't even like!"

"Enough. Not another word. I forbid you to see him again."

Dear Diary,

My mother and I are avoiding each other. At the store, I catch Dad looking at me, and sadly shaking his head. On the nights Mom goes to the Methodist church to roll bandages, I've been staying late and helping Dad straighten the stock and sweep.

It was almost dark tonight when I saw Karl outside the store. I told Dad that Elaine and Mary Lou were waiting for me to go bowling, and before he could stop me, I ran out, met Karl around the corner, and we drove out to the lake.

"Now," I thought, "I'll talk to him about Lilly. He'll listen. He'll have to!"

He parked in back of the dance hall. Inside, the jukebox was playing "That Old Black Magic." He started to help me into the back of his truck.

"That old black magic has me in its spell . . ." And suddenly, I didn't want to talk. I didn't even want to neck. Not just yet. I told him I wanted to dance.

". . . I should stay away, but what can I do?"

He just looked at me.

"C'mon. Please, Karl?"

"Oh, okay." He didn't look happy.

The song was over. We stood at the jukebox and studied the dozens of choices. Finally, Karl grinned, dropped a nickel into the slot, and Frank Sinatra's voice billowed out. "I'll be seeing you . . ."

My heart skipped. He remembered!

We stepped onto the scuffed wooden floor. He held me very close. We were the only ones on the floor.

I reached up and stroked his blond head; we smiled, he slipped his leg between mine. A bunch of kids burst into the hall. Karl said, "Let's get out of here."

Outside, we climbed into the back of his truck. He'd prepared, no more stinking feed sacks anymore; we lay down on a blanket.

Inside the hall, someone put in another nickel. "All Of Me . . ."

Karl pulled off his shirt.

"Why not take all of me . . ." He kicked off his pants. I closed my eyes.

I let him undo my blouse—unfasten my bra—let him pull off my skirt—let him slip off my underpants. And then there was nothing between us; his strong smooth body was clamped onto mine. My heart was going a mile a minute.

He touched me. ". . . So why not take all of me . . ."

"Oh, Karl." I wanted us to be one person. I did!

"Oh!"

I couldn't! I jerked myself away.

"No!" I sat up. I couldn't!

I couldn't take a chance and do it!

I found Dad waiting up for me. Next to his easy chair, his ashtray was overflowing with cigarette stubs.

He looked up at me. He said he could tell I hadn't been bowling. He said that he knew it wasn't possible to watch me every minute. He said that he would like to know what I saw in Karl. "Your mother and I . . . his family . . . we don't think . . . suitable . . . he's not."

What did I see in him? Not suitable? I love him, that's all! He fills the big, empty space in my heart, that's all!

Without a word I stomped up to my room.

Karl, it's 2:00 a.m. I could tell you were really disappointed when I pulled my clothes back on, I guess I really let you down. But you didn't put that thing—you know what I mean—a rubber—on you. And I did tell you that I was afraid to take a chance. I'm too young to have a baby, Karl—or to have to get rid of a baby. I couldn't do it.

Oh, God, now it's 4:00 a.m. Maybe Karl and I should go bowling for a change. Or take a walk. Or sit in the top row of the balcony at the Royal and smooch while watching a smoochy movie. Or go canoeing. Maybe I'd even take him to that narrow passageway. Maybe I'd even take him to my island.

Is it Karl I really love? Or is it his kisses? Whatever it is, I can't give up on him. I've got to make him understand.

Dear Diary,

As soon as the front door closed after my parents, I heard the mailman ring. I clunked downstairs and found a V-mail letter.

Dear Janet,

I am writing to you from a secret place in Europe. I have been thinking about you and I want to answer your letter while I can. I don't know if Lilly was named after the lily of the valley, but she did love to seek them out in the forest near our home. And Lilly did love to draw. She loved to dance. She loved to sing.

What was hardest for Lilly to bear was her lifelong friends deserting her. They carried on with school, and their clubs and parties without her. My heart was harder, I told myself I did not care, but Lilly . . . she kept asking what she could have done wrong, why was she being punished. My poor little innocent sister who loved painting and singing and dancing and the moon; she could not understand any of it.

I cannot keep it inside of me any longer, Janet. I don't know how, but I know for certain that Lilly is dead. Murdered by people of my country. By the Nazis.

If only she could have come with me to America. If only she could have escaped, even to the moon. She was so alive. Such an alive person. As you are so alive, Janet. As you are so kind and good.

I have pinned the photograph of you on the wall next to my army cot. Please, Janet. Take good care of yourself. I hope we can see each other when the war is over.

Always yours,
Rudi

P.S. I love the drawing you did of Lilly in the lily of the valley. I will always treasure it. Thank you for thinking about her.

So it's true. It really happened.
She's really lost. Really dead.

I'm making myself sit still. Making myself write back to Rudi.

Dear Rudi,
Thank you for your letter.

Dear Rudi
Lilly and I have so much in common . . . .

Dear Rudi
I'm so, so sorry . . . .

Dear Rudi,
We can't give up hope. Maybe it's not true, maybe it's just a horrible nightmare. Maybe now that you're a soldier . . . now that you're in Europe again in a United States of America uniform, you'll find her and send her here. It is possible, isn't it? I'll rush to Ellis Island and bring her home with me on the train. We'll practice English together and I'll teach her all the latest Hit Parade songs and how to jitterbug if she doesn't already know how . . .

I threw down my pencil, ran to the window and inhaled the cool green of Mrs. Dickerson's elm tree.

It didn't help.

Still in my nightgown, I ran across the street. At the school playground I grabbed a swing and pumped. The sun was on my face, the sky blazed blue, my shadow below me kept swinging, swinging.

I pumped harder. I pumped as high and hard as I could.

I pumped till I almost flew over the top.

Dear Diary,

Another letter. I ripped open the pink envelope.

> *Dear little Janet,*
>
> *I expected to hear from you by now. The big news here is that Gamma Delta Gamma is getting ready for pledge week. I hope we get some freshman girls that are as cute as you. My other news is that I've thrown over the boyfriend I told you about. Now I'm going with the darlingest Sigma Chi man; it's the best fraternity.*
>
> *How are you doing with Karl? Write back.*
>
> *XX Connie*

I wanted to scream.

I did scream. Not just at her. At me, too. I hated her. I hated myself. For never standing up to her. For wanting to be her friend so bad. The picture I made of her, so pretty, so perfect smile, so perfect teeth, so perfect tiny waist, so perfectly hideous inside.

I ran into the bathroom, closed the door, slammed shut the window—I didn't want to scare the whole town—and screamed bloody murder.

I ripped up the envelope. I tore the letter into tiny jagged pieces. I flushed her and her letter down the toilet.

Dear Poor Old Diary,

It's 4:30 a.m. I just charged over to the window and stuck my face in Mrs. Dickerson's tree. It went on like a horrible movie. I'm still in a shivery sweat.

I was somewhere in Europe. On some war front, I think. The old man with a long white beard came toward me. Was it my grandfather? No. He said he was Karl's grandfather. Was I supposed to save him? Then the old man and I were looking up into a tree. A pale new moon hung over the tree. The old man kept shaking the tree and I said, why are you doing that, and then I saw a baby robin fly out. But it wasn't a robin; it was a tiny girl dressed in white. She seemed to be trying to fly up to the moon. I called, Lilly, come down here, and she looked down and smiled like she knew me and spread out her arms. But she had no wings. I just stood there with my mouth hanging open and my own arms at my sides, and she fell to the ground and blood spurted out of her neck. I ran to the Statue of Liberty for help but it towered over me with Connie's face and screeched, get out, what are you doing here? Don't you know you can't belong to Gamma Gamma Gamma gamma gamma . . .

The robins have begun their morning, "Cheer up, cheer up, cheer up." The pale morning light is seeping into the sky. A fading, almost full moon is hanging over the tree.

Dear Diary,

Dad and I worked late tonight, marking stock and sweeping up. Starting for home up Main Street, I looked up at the moon sliding out from behind the clouds. Dad looked up, too, and smiled.

"So beautiful it is," he said. "So beautiful, my Janet."

I turned and peered at him.

"I was just remembering," he told me. "My friends and myself, when

I was your age, we climbed a hill near our village for to watch the moon come up."

I tucked my arm in his.

"Dad." It slipped out. "Did you ever want to escape to the moon?"

He stopped and stared at me. "Of a thing like that! What made you think of such a crazy thing?"

"Oh, I don't know. It was just a thought. But did you?"

"No, honey." He took my hand. "Where else but right here on this beautiful little piece of Mother Earth would I want to live? Besides, where else but in this good little town could I be friends with the Chief of Police and the Mayor?" He laughed and went on about how here in America the streets aren't paved with gold as they were told in the Old Country but if you worked hard and were honest, every person had the same right to be happy, the same chance to succeed.

We crossed over the bridge and started up River Street. The moon, shining down, seemed to follow us. My dad kept his hand over mine.

We were almost home.

"But Dad, did you ever have any problems with people? Did anyone ever do something bad to you when you were a kid?"

I watched him bend, strike a match on his shoe, and light a cigarette, He gave a short laugh. "No."

"Really? Are you sure, Dad?"

"I am sure, of course. Anyone, why should they do anything bad to me?"

We walked on in silence, turned left on our block.

"But Dad," I had to keep on, "what about Mom's family? I never heard . . ."

After a minute, "There were, my Janet, for your mother's family, many hardships . . . a hard life . . . many troubles."

Yes. I know. Pogroms.

"Also, in the Great War the Poles invaded them, also the Germans."

Dad's smile looked crooked. "Of those German soldiers, those who stole potatoes from your mother's garden, just think, one of them, he could have been me."

The crickets loudly proclaimed their territories. Mrs. Dickerson's elm tree rustled; its tall silhouette was charcoal-dark against the dark sky.

We stood outside our house.

"That we live here in Elksburg, you're happy about it, aren't you, honey?"

"Of course." I squeezed his hand. "But what about before you came to this country? I want to know more about you when you were a kid."

He didn't seem to hear me, only lit another cigarette.

Dad, you never answer my questions."

He yawned and looked at his watch. "It is late. Tomorow is another work day."

"Yes, I know."

He looked at me. "You want to know about my family. Not much is there to say. But your mother," my dad's voice grew soft, "she came to this country, like me, for to seek a better life." He drew hard on his cigarette. "One thing always you must remember, my daughter. If anything bad should ever happen, if life sometimes brings pain, it is time that will heal it. Remember that, my Janet. Time heals all wounds, all pain."

Another of his catch-all sayings.

I don't believe a word of it. I don't believe that time has healed pain for my mother. Or for my poor, sad dad.

Dear Diary,

I finally got up the courage to write back to Rudi. But not about what I'm thinking. That Aunt Pearl was wrong when she said she thought Lilly was caught when she was out looking for food. No, I can see it in my head—Lilly was caught when she was out in the forest looking for lilies of the valley. It was night and she was watching the moon slide out from behind some clouds and they shot her there and she screamed and fell and died alone and her body lay there and got picked over and eaten by scavenging animals and now she's just a small white skeleton lying under some moldy leaves.

I only wrote to Rudi about how terribly sorry I am about Lilly. Only how I feel I've lost someone close to me. Only that I'll never forget her. Only how I'll always be his friend.

Nothing about how wrong he is about me, thinking that I'm such a good person.

And then, I wrote a letter to perfectly hideous Connie.

> *Inside your perfectly perfect body you are ugly! signed from your very former and very Jewish friend.*

A very short and very hideously, perfectly true letter.

Dear Diary,

I got a phone call from Mary Lou. Karl wants to meet me at the A&W; there's some kind of get-together.

Mom watched me from the kitchen table. I held the phone closer to my ear. "Thanks, Mary Lou," I said, "I'd love to get together with just us girls tonight."

"What?" Mary Lou said. "Oh, okay, I get it. I'll tell Elaine."

Dear friend Diary, the world may be lousy but my friends are still loyal. I still love Karl. And I'm going to show up at the A&W tonight.

Here goes, Dear Diary,

Maybe you already suspected it and you're sick and tired of it by now. Sick and tired of stupid me. I sure am. Goddamn, deadly sick. But here it is.

Soon after Mary Lou called, she and Elaine were at the door. Dad told us to go and have a good time.

Mom gave me the eagle eye and said, "Be home by eleven."

Outside, a full moon broke out from behind some clouds. I hurried my friends away and we ran all six blocks to the A&W.

The place was packed. Karl was wearing a blue shirt that matched his eyes. We sat at a long table with the others; a big change from the two of us lying in the back of his truck. Elaine and Mary Lou kept telling everyone how great I was at drawing faces. "It's like magic," Elaine kept on. "Really! You should see the way she can capture a person on paper." Karl spoke up, too. "She's the best."

I squeezed his hand as Mary Lou whipped out a drawing pad, and Elaine handed me some pencils. My friends really did want to show me off.

Being the center of attention felt funny at first—everyone wanted to pose for me—but I soon settled down to it. Under the table, Karl pressed his knee against mine.

And then Morrie Fitzgerald swaggered in. He saw the kids crowded around me. "Get a load of her!" he spouted. "Thinks she's pretty hot potatoes, don't she?"

Someone said, "You're drunk, Morrie."

"So you went to a fancy art school in Milwaukee." He bent over me; I could smell his sour-alcohol breath. "So you think you're a big shot!"

My hand shook a little.

"So you think you're better'n us!"

My friends yelled, "Cut it out, Morrie!"

I kept my head down. Concentrate on the eyes, I told myself. Concentrate on the nose, the lips, the shape of the face . . . the humanity . . .

"That's a show-off Jew for you!"

My head spun. My stomach churned.

I went hot, then cold.

I looked at Karl. He just sat there.

I got up. It was like slow motion.

I hit Morrie in the face.

He gasped. Everyone gasped.

Karl got up. He took hold of Morrie's arm. He led him away.

I ran out the door. Elaine and Mary Lou yelled, "Wait for us!" and ran after me.

I ran faster. Through quiet, tree-lined neighborhoods with the city hall clock chiming, ran past the high school and poor Mr. Stubenbaker's house, and Emil Wilson's house, past neighbors' lighted front windows and neighbors sitting around their radios. I zigzagged through neighbors' backyards, crashed into Mrs. Dickerson's garden, and cut myself on her rosebushes. I walked around the block to catch my breath.

Then I walked in the front door.

Dad looked up, surprised. "So early you are home?"

Before my mother could read my mind, I said, "Nothing's wrong, Mom. I just need to get some sleep."

"Your leg, you're bleeding!"

"It's nothing, Mom."

I went into the bathroom and cleaned off the blood. Then I climbed as calmly, and slowly, and steadily as I could up the stairs to my room.

I stared at my wall full of drawings of birds and dragonflies and

Frank Sinatra. I stared at Karl on my mirror, at my shelves full of drawing pads and scrapbooks since I was five. I stared at Heidi with its beautiful cover showing Heidi and her grandfather.

Why didn't he hit Morrie? Why did he help Morrie instead of me?

Downstairs, the phone rang. I pulled the pillow over my head.

Dear Poor, Poor, Old Diary,

My parents have left for the store; the phone is ringing. He's calling again. He's going to explain why he didn't come after me. He's going to apologize for not hitting Morrie himself.

It was Mary Lou.

"Elaine and I couldn't catch up with you last night. We called you up and your mom said you were sleeping."

I didn't say anything.

"Janet, are you still there?

"I'm here."

"That Fitzgerald is a scumbag," she said. "You're not going to pay attention to a sleazy nothing like him, are you?"

I was silent.

"Forget what he said. He's not worth getting into a stew over. As for Karl . . ."

"I have to go." I hung up.

A blast of the doorbell.

It was him.

I stared at him. "What do you want?"

"I want to know why you got so worked up and ran out on me last night."

I couldn't believe my ears. "Didn't you hear what your buddy said?"

"Oh, you know old Morrie. He always says stupid things when he's drunk."

"Stupid things? Didn't you see how hurt I was? Why didn't you say anything? Why didn't you help me instead of him?"

"I don't know." Karl turned red. "Let's just forget it."

"Forget it? You're asking me to forget it?"

"Aw, Janet. I would think . . . I would think you'd just be glad I overlook it."

"Overlook what?"

He shifted from one foot to the other.

"Overlook what?"

"Oh, c'mon, Janet. You know. Your folks and all . . ."

I didn't move.

"Oh, you know. I mean, I think I've been doing a good job."

"A good job?"

"You know."

"No, I don't know.

"You know, a good job of overlooking you being Jewish."

Was I hearing right? "Overlooking my being Jewish?"

"C'mon, Janet," he took a step back. "You know. Anyway, you're different from . . . I mean, you could always change, you could become Lutheran. Besides, you're probably adopted, you don't even look like a . . ."

I slammed the door in his face.

I know. It could be much worse. I could be a poor refugee. I could be Lilly, I could be dead. But I feel all dead inside. Please God, help me. Oh what a fool I am. Asking for help when nothing will help.

Tonight Dad tapped at my door and said I'd been hiding in my room all day and that it was long enough. "My Janet, come down please. Your supper, your mother has made meatloaf; it is on the table."

"I'm not hungry."

"My Janet . . ."

At last I heard his slow tread going down the stairs.

I could tell from the way Mom knocked that she knew. After all, she has eyes in the back of her head. "Janet . . ." Her voice was low. "Daughter . . ."

I didn't answer.

Finally, she went away, too.

I'm a nurse in Europe, deep in the fighting zone, desperately trying to save the wounded, even giving them my own blood. By some miracle Karl appears just as I die a horrible death and he lives with never-ending guilt the rest of his life

I find Karl's grandfather who turns out to be a Nazi, but I save him anyway. Karl parachutes down, realizes what I've done and asks me to forgive him but I say goodbye to him forever and walk off into the mist with Rudi and Lilly.

Oh, God.

Dear Old Friend Diary,

This morning Dad knocked on my door and said that my friends were asking for me. I told him to go away.

I almost have to laugh when I think of how this diary began, of what an idiot I've been most of this summer, hoping for one of those ultraromantic, "against-all-odds, happily-ever-after" movie endings.

I found out how to lose weight. Don't eat for two and a half days; I look skinny in the mirror.

Lilly is back on my mirror. Lilly still looks the same.

She'll always look the same. She'll never fall in love, never write another line of poetry, never march in a band, never grow up. Never search for lilies of the valley. Never see herself in a mirror, skinny or any other way.

I found some letters under my door.

From Elaine:

> *Dearest darling Jannie,*
> *Band practice tomorrow. We're going to learn some new and exciting maneuvers for halftimes at the football games in September. We need you.*

From Mary Lou:

> *Dear best and cutest pal in the world,*
> *There's going to be a dance with a real band out at the lake in a few days. It'll be our last fling before school starts and there's a rumor that a bunch of sailors will be there. My mom said she"ll drive us and I'm going to dare you to wink at the cutest guy.*

A knock. Without waiting, my mother let herself in.

"You're not hungry?"

Yes. I shook my head. "No."

"Janet," my mother's hands twisted together, "I have something to tell you. Something that happened to me in the old country. When I was younger than you. I didn't want to ever tell you, didn't want you to ever know. Your father and I, we wanted you to grow up happy, without any troubles."

I stared at her. My silent mother took a breath and blurted, "I was hurt." Her eyes, staring back at me, filled with tears; her face crumpled, "The men . . . It was bad . . ."

And I knew. What my aunt tried to tell me when she said young girls were assaulted. What my dad couldn't say. There was a Pogrom. My mother was attacked . . . raped . . . by Russian Cossacks.

Mom was already out the door with, "I have alterations to finish at the store."

I felt numb. After a minute, I followed her downstairs. She was already gone.

I read the note on the kitchen table. Dear Daughter, I have made you something. I hope you like it, With Love, from your mother

On the oilcloth was a whole apple pie with cheddar cheese.

Dear Diary,

It's an hour later and Dad walked into the house. His eyes lit up to see that I wasn't still holed up in my room. He asked me what he could do for me. "Just ask me, please. I will get it for you."

All at once I knew. "I want to go to the lake."

He looked surprised. But, good old Daddy, he didn't ask any more questions. Except that he wouldn't agree to take me till I practically swore on a bible that I wasn't going to do away with myself.

I packed a slice of the apple pie and the cheese in wax paper, a sketchbook and pencils, and you, in my knapsack, and we drove out to Eagle Lake. Dad said he'd pick me up at Dicky's Dock in three hours.

He watched me paddle off from the dock. I looked back at him and waved.

So now you know, Dear Diary, that I'm writing this on my secret island. The sky is still blue, the clouds are still pure white, the water is still silky-smooth. The only sounds are the soft lapping of the water on the shore and the sighing of wind in the trees. A white egret is standing motionless on the shore.

It feels as if I've been gone for a very long time.

It feels as if I haven't taken a deep breath for a very long time.

Everything's the same.

And everything's changed.

It's not only about Karl Kunkel, anymore. Though I know I'm never going to forget what happened with him this summer. It's about the war and Rudi and Lilly. About people despised for being different. Despised just for being who they are.

And it's about my mother; all these years afraid to tell me about her past. And terrified for me. And it's about me—who's been afraid to be who I am.

Tonight we'll talk. I'll show my parents the picture of Lilly. I'll tell them about her, tell them about Rudi and that I know what's happening to people like us in Europe. I'll tell them they don't have to protect me anymore, they don't have to hide the truth from me anymore.

I'll tell them there's a lot I need to know.

And, oh, Dear Diary, here comes a lone dragonfly. Maybe the same dragonfly. Maybe the last dragonfly of summer, as clear and beautiful as blue stained glass. Buzzing around me again. Staring at me with his many eyes.

I grabbed my pencil and I'm pressing down hard.

No more keeping quiet!

No more hiding who I am!

I'll be different all right.

I'll be as different as I want to be!

I'm so different I dumped him!

My pencil keeps moving. I draw the dragonfly. I draw my dad as a boy, looking up at the moon. I draw Mom, young and pretty, and on the next page, I make her surrounded by friends. I draw Mrs. Dickerson, and the lady dwarf, and Pop Ritterband, and the Negro soldier on the train. I draw my friends and my imaginary grandfather high in the mountains of Switzerland.

Bright yellow aspen leaves are spinning and falling. I keep drawing, keep turning the pages. I draw Lilly and me, each cradling a baby robin, and Rudi and me in a canoe. I sketch my mother and me smiling at each other.

I draw the lilies of the valley right under where I'm sitting, waiting for next spring.

A low light is over everything. The soft end-of-summer wind is touching my cheek. The tree's shadow and my shadow are spread long together over the ground.

I'm holding my sketchbook to my chest, to my lips.

The thread is here.

And now, Dear Diary, I'm going to draw a portrait of me.

Me, so far.

Me, Janet Kessler, one little drop in the ocean.

On this tiny speck on the planet.

Alone, under this tree.

Just me.

With my eyes looking out at this dark and dangerous . . . and beautiful . . . world.

AFTERWORD

In 1943, incredible as it seems, what news there was about the Holocaust was hidden in back pages of newspapers in the United States. Whatever horror was reported was not believed by the general public. Only in 1945, after the Allies won the war, did Americans find out that the Nazis had murdered six million Jewish men, women, and children, as well as millions of others deemed inferior. During this same period, racism and anti-Semitism were alive and well in the United States.

These words, written by Hillel more that two thousand years ago, are as important for us today as there were 2000 years ago.

I get up
I walk.
I fall down.
Meanwhile, I keep dancing.

Hillel, Jewish rabbi and scholar
60 B.C.E.-10 C.E.

ABOUT THE AUTHOR

A graduate in art education from the University of Wisconsin, Madiison, Ruth Lercher Bornstein has had ten one person exhibits and has participated in many more. "I thought painting what I needed to say was enough for one lifetime," Ruth says, "until I grew my first vegetable garden. Suddenly words became as real to me as paint."

Ruth is author of the novel, *Butterflies and Lizards, Beryl and Me* and a book of essays, titled *The Sky and Me*, as well author/illustrator of fifteen children's books, including *Little Gorilla, Rabbits Good News,* and *The Dancing Man*. She is also illustrator of six additional books. Ruth has taught "Creating the Picture Book" at the university of California, Los Angles Extension and is a two-time winner of the Southern California Council on Children's Literature Award for Illustration.

For more information visit ruthlercherbornstein.com
or wellstonepress.com